Mata Hari
One Life for Another

By
D. Alan Lewis

Mata Hari

One Life for Another

Copyright © 2021 D. Alan Lewis

All rights reserved. No part of this book may be reproduced, duplicated, copied, or transmitted in any form or by any means without the express written consent and permission of the author.

This is a work of fiction. The names, characters, places, and incidents are fictitious or are used fictitiously. Any resemblance to any person or persons, living or dead, is purely coincidental.

Published by D. Alan Lewis
and
Voodoo Rumors Media

Interior and cover design by D. Alan Lewis
Cover model: Sara Neathery
Edited by Mia Mellette

Voodoo Rumors Media
Nashville, Tennessee 37211

Part One: A Dancer's Secret

Paris, France
May 1916

They sat and watched in awe as the goddess arose through the smoke, appearing in a storm of sparkling light on the stage before them. Her hands and arms, curling and unfolding in wave-like motions, moved in rhythmic concert with her hips and torso. The dance, learned in the Orient and perfected here in her private dance hall, was meant to mesmerize and enthrall the strongest of wills, from the simple-minded Parisian elite to the war-weary Allied officers. The cozy little hall only seated twenty at tables arranged in a semi-circle. Every chair was meticulously placed so every eye would be on her.

The goddess wanted them close to her as the champagne flowed and her hypnotic dance kept them enchanted. The oils and perfume she wore smelled rich and exotic. As her hands waved in the direction of the onlookers, the scents traveled out like invisible tentacles, enveloping the unsuspecting with her addicting aroma.

As she moved around the stage, the dancer kept a certain man in view. He looked too young and naïve to be so perfectly placed as an attaché to General Gouraud, Commander of the French Fourth Army. A smile formed on her painted lips as the lieutenant sat spellbound, his eyes obviously drinking in the alluring sight of her, just as she had planned.

She already knew his name was Archard Bonnay, newly assigned to the General's staff. His dark hair contrasted with his pale complexion. His spotless uniform, so neatly pressed, only served to make him look younger than his nineteen years. While many of the General's staff attended her performances, even if only on occasion, his invitation to this evening's performance was not by chance. Dancing was only the prelude to the darker performance she planned. The new thrall to the goddess would be the subject of this evening's work.

If the gods can't resist me, what hope is there for these mere mortals? She smiled internally at the thought, but her face never changed nor did her movements stray from the well-practiced routine.

Despite the movements of her dance, the fog of sweet-smelling incense, rising from the scores of lit joss sticks posed along the back of the stage, appeared undisturbed. The ribbons of white smoke lifted into the rafters and rippled across the ceiling before falling downward and flooding the performance hall with their scent.

The patrons had paid dearly for a chance to see the erotic mysteries of her Oriental dancing, a form of worship to the gods of the East. That is what she liked them to think. Her seductive tribute to the foreign deities allowed their minds to open, so that by the end of the night, her level of worship seemed diminished by the patrons' worship of her.

She swayed to the beating of drums, moving back and forth with her arms outstretched, hands and fingers flexing, beckoning, directing every eye's focus to her. Like obedient pets, they all sat, unmoving thralls to her every whim, to her every movement, to her every desire. Men wanted her, as did many of the women, who occasionally shifted in their seats, unused to the unfamiliar stirring within.

She thrived in her element, this world she had created for herself. Some called her a goddess, but she preferred the name she had forged for herself.

Mata Hari, Eye of the Dawn.

The stage glowed, illuminated by the spotlights hanging from the ceiling and shining their colored light directly down, leaving shadows here and there, as well as brightly punctuated patches of brilliance for her to dance through. The intensity of the bulbs' light reflected off her jeweled garments, dazzling the eyes and occasionally falling upon the darkened audience. Pinpoints of luminescence moved throughout the hall in concert with her movements, going where she deemed. To her admirers, she had mastered not only the pathway into their hearts and minds, but the very elements of nature itself.

Her thin silk skirt became all but transparent under the focus of the brighter lights, offering hints of the treasure which lay beneath, and causing excited spikes in the heartbeats of those few who sat close enough to discern the details.

As she spun, Mata gave her manager and confidante, Oscar, a subtle smirk and nod, letting him know that she saw the surrender in the lieutenant's eyes. She would break him in the usual manner.

The man nodded his understanding to his Mistress. Mata knew that before the performance ended, Oscar would inform the young lieutenant that the goddess wished an audience with him in her chambers.

With the last dance of the evening complete, the

exhausted woman retired to her chambers on the floor above the performance hall. Disrobing, she dipped a toe into the newly drawn bath. The cool water felt more than welcome since the sweltering heat of the Parisian summer remained in the room even this late into the evening. Leaning back, she allowed herself a few moments of blissful silence in the bubbly water. The day had been filled with hours of practice and prep work getting the hall set up, followed by the performance itself. Mata need this time to herself to collect her thoughts.

An image of the young lieutenant came to mind. He was just a boy, full of lust, desire, and unbridled energy; a boy whom she intended to make into a man this evening. Her mind played on the different ways the night could begin and progress. Oh, the things she could do to him or that he could do to her.

It was only when the first movement of her fingertip across her plump pink pearl occurred, that she realized her hands had snaked down between her thighs. With eyes closed so she could see her future lover better, Mata sank into the pleasures of the moment. The first touch of her finger quickly became the first of many as thoughts of herself being in his arms, feeling his hot breath on her neck, and opening herself to his steady yet firm thrusts, her hand moved faster, whipping the water of the bath into a soapy frenzy. Unable to resist the impending release, she moaned a name.

It was not the young man's name. Instead, the face and name shifted into that of the only man who had ever come close to taming her. So many times, he had tried to tame her but, in the end, she broke him. Thoughts of her beloved General, on top of her and yielding his soul and seed to her, sent her over the edge. She cried out his name as her back arched. Every muscle in her body seemed to contract at once as the little death claimed her. For what seemed like an eternity, her body shuddered as her fingers refused to stop, drawing out a second and then a third climax. Over and over, Mata cried out the name and with it, her body reacted. She felt herself being drained of resistance, wanting nothing more than to have the orgasms continue.

When her hands finally withdrew, she felt herself drop back into the tub, falling in more ways than one. Smiling, she let the images slowly fade away.

"As always, my beautiful Otto. Thank you for never failing me," she whispered.

After catching her breath, she remembered the time. With haste, she snatched her rose-scented soap and began removing the layers of white talc she had applied before the final dance to give her body the pale and unearthly appearance of the Hindu goddess Maya.

Stories of Maya portrayed her as a goddess of illusion. It was said that she created the material world to occupy humanity so they would not see the deeper spiritual truths of the universe. Mata tried to honor the goddess, since she felt she was an incarnation of the divine illusionist. Like Maya, she danced to distract men from the truth of who she really was.

Hearing the front door open and footfalls approaching, she rinsed off and stood. Her eyes moved to the bathroom's open doorway as Oscar appeared. Without modesty, she turned to face him. Mata enjoyed having the older man, as well as anyone else, seeing her nude. In those moments, she was the center of attention. His face glowed and a smile appeared on his weathered face. She never tired of making him smile, considering all he did for her as caretaker of the performance hall and her personal servant.

Mata watched his eyes move as he looked her over, gleaning every detail. She started to speak but decided to let him watch the water and the remaining soap bubbles as they ran down the length of her form. The dirty old pervert was far too old for her to play with, but his loyal service did deserve some form of reward, over and above his usual share of the box office profits. Tilting her head, she gave him a knowing smile and grabbed a towel to dry off with.

He cleared his throat and said in a frail voice, "Madame, the lieutenant is in the hallway. Shall I send him in?"

Stepping from the tub, she tossed the towel toward him. "Dry my back for me, please. And grab my robe from the nightstand." She turned her back to him as he approached. "Tell me more about the boy."

Lightly running the cloth across her back, Oscar began telling her what she needed to know before the evening's work began.

"From what our friends in the High Command have told me, Archard Bonnay is well placed within Gouraud's staff." He squatted down and wiped the soapy water from her thighs and then took a deep breath as he moved the towel up, running it over the curves of her backside. "We, um... How long do you think we can continue playing both sides in this war before…"?

She turned slightly to look down at him as he glanced up to meet her gaze. He immediately silenced his tongue. He knew his place well. Giving a slight nod, he lowered his eyes and continued toweling her dry.

"Dear Oscar, neither Walter nor Georges would let me come to harm, even if their subordinates caught on to my… little games." Mata said and looked back down, then abruptly turned. "Make sure to pay attention to my nethers. My new soap is wonderful on my skin but a bother down there, if left for too long."

She heard him sigh and giggled. Mata did enjoy toying with him, almost as much as he loved being teased. The old man looked up, and she watched as he became lost in her dark bewitching eyes.

Like him, Mata knew her overconfidence in those opposing spymasters would eventually catch up to her. She only hoped the Great War would end before that time came. She wanted to curse the two men who had recruited her into this dangerous profession, one German and the other French. But really, she only had herself to blame. She'd agreed to spy for both sides because it gave her what she craved the most; power over the men who ran things on the battlefront, power over the men in the governments, and all those secretive powerbrokers who pulled the strings, behind the scenes.

Walter Nicolai worked as the Chief of Section III B of the German military's Kriegsnachrichtenstelle West. He thought she might be a spy, given her travels through Europe in the early days of the conflict, and threatened her with imprisonment, a year earlier. But a single night alone with Walter convinced him otherwise. He realized that her skills would be perfect for someone engaging in a life of espionage. Mata agreed to his request to spy for the Keizer and had quickly become one of Germany's top agents in France, supplying them with ample amounts

7

of high-level secrets on both French and British operations.

Then, just a matter of months ago, Captain Georges Ladoux of the French intelligence organization, the Deuxième Bureau de l'État, had drawn her into his clutches and convinced her to spy for him as a double agent. With the Americans soon to enter the fray, she would have to find a way to dance her way into the heart of their commander, a man they called Blackjack.

Despite her years living in Paris, she still retained her Dutch citizenship, and with her homeland remaining neutral in the continental struggle, it allowed her free passage between the Allied and Axis nations. This advantage made a perfect arrangement for her work as a dancer, performer, and a spy, although she preferred the term, provocatrix.

With a subtle gesture, Oscar stood and laid the towel over his shoulder. Mata stepped close and kissed him on the forehead.

"Give me a moment to dab some perfume on and then send the young man in," she purred. Mata walked away from the man, leaving him to watch the sway of her bare hips as she crossed the room. Turning, she smiled, knowing he was totally hers to play with. "Take care of the receipts downstairs and then you can lock up. And don't worry about tonight, I'll be fine alone with my... prey." Pointing to his crotch, she added. "Take care of that little thing tonight as you think of me."

"Yes, Madame," Oscar said, almost swooning.

She watched his reflection in the mirror of her vanity as he took one more look at her nude form. Wiggling her hips before he turned away, she said, "Go on, mon chéri. I have work to do and a man to ruin for all other women." She smiled.

Mata slid on her robe as knuckles rapped at the door.

"Enter," she said in a commanding but compassionate voice.

Lieutenant Bonnay stuck his head into the dimly lit but lavishly decorated apartment. His gaze moved around, taking in the wonderful mixture of Western and Oriental décor. Tiny flames illuminated the room, and scented oils within the candles filled the air with the smells of lavender and sandalwood.

Parting the translucent curtains that draped her bedroom's doorway on the far side of the room, she stepped into the room. The young man skipped a breath, his eyes wide and drinking in the sight of her. With her dancing attire gone, only a silky red robe covered her slim form, falling open all the way down to her waist and giving the young man an ample view.

"Bonsoir, Madame," he said.

"Come inside. Relax and sit with me, mon chéri," she purred and moved to the pillow-covered divan.

Mata felt his eyes studying her as she sat and leaned back into the plush cushions. For a moment, she forgot the man and just enjoyed being off her feet. For a woman nearing her fortieth year, remembering the elaborate dance movements still came easy, but each month the physical demands of the performances seemed to exact a heavier toll.

Looking him up and down, she bit her tongue at the thought of the firm physique beneath the uniform. She may be tired, but a good lover always perked her up.

She looked up at his eyes as they studied the movements of her breasts, gently rocking as she seductively rolled her shoulders beneath the silk until another prize came into view. The lower portion of her robe opened just enough to allow the thick black curls of her sex to be seen. The view didn't happen by accident and she allowed it long enough to ensure his gaze fell upon it.

Give them a glimpse and whet their appetites, she thought.

Then, with a twist of her hips and a shift of her thigh, she took it away and denied him the view. An expression of despair crashed down on him, making her think of a sad puppy.

"Why don't you pour us a drink?" she said and gestured to a bamboo liquor cabinet.

"Yes, Madame." Rushing to it, he opened both cabinet doors and looked at the selection. Picking up a bottle, he turned and asked, "Irish whiskey?"

"Excellent choice, but only a little for me." She watched him pour.

Although she did like her drink, Mata had no desire to let the alcohol diminish her skills tonight, and truth be told, she preferred that he did not drink too much either. Although a drunk or even tipsy man would be more likely to spill secrets to her, she enjoyed the challenge of breaking him with her sensuality and skills alone.

"This is hard to come by these days. The Irish distilleries have been silenced due to the food rationing in the UK," he said, handing her the glass with a finger's worth of the amber fluid.

"I have a dear friend in Dublin, and I had the opportunity to travel there last year with him. I always bring home a case or two when I return." She took a sip and looked into his eyes. "When I saw you from the stage, I found myself wanting to know you better."

His eyes widened and a strange smile formed, as if questioning her words. She reached over, letting her fingertips brush across his cheek.

"You have a certain look, like a young animal ready for his first conquest. I like that look, a look of a man brimming with unbridled passion. Have you ever...?"

He blushed. "There were a couple of girls that lived near the farm I grew up on."

She leaned closer, letting him smell the alcohol on her breath and the perfume on her neck. Speaking in a seductive whisper, Mata asked, "Did you deflower them? Both of them? Claim their virginity as your own?"

Her lips fell lightly on his cheek and slowly kissed again and again, moving towards his neck. He moaned and answered her question with a slight nodded, letting his eyes close in expectation of the coming kiss.

"Good boy."

Her hand brushed along his cheek again and then snaked behind his head. There was no resistance as she pulled him to her, pressing her lips to his.

The pair kissed and talked for half an hour. Mata nudged the conversation this way and that to glean his experiences and what most excited him sexually. More than once, she had to restrain his hands as they wandered beneath the silk.

Sliding to the edge of the lounge, Mata took his hands and stood, drawing him up as well. Keeping his hands in hers, she walked backwards, so that their eyes never looked away from one another. As they passed through the silk curtain, he pulled his hands away and began to unbutton his jacket.

"No, no, mon'amour. Let me." She pulled his hand down to his sides and stepped close as she began to undress him. He stood a few inches taller than her, a trait she approved of in her men. "Pour moi, undressing a lover is like unwrapping a present on Christmas morning." The jacket fell to the floor, followed quickly by his tie and shirt.

Mata smiled as she indulged herself and ran a finger across his bare chest, running it down to his waistline. She pulled him closer, standing on her toes, so their lips met again for a brief kiss. Then Mata dropped to her knees and began to finish what she had started. In short order, his boots and pants were gone, leaving the young man nude. Reaching up, she gently wrapped her fingers around his manhood and pulled it up towards her face. She tilted it one way then another, before looking up and locking eyes with him. The throbbing of it brought a satisfying smile to her face. Leaning closer, she blew through pursed lips, onto the tip of it. His eyes closed and a moan escaped him.

Carefully, she opened her mouth, letting her tongue brush against the tip, circling around it until she felt the throbbing intensify. He moaned again and she rewarded his appreciation with a deliberately slow lick along the underside of the head.

She straightened and then jumped up to her feet, surprising him. Taking his hands, she eased him onto her bed. Expensive silk sheets and pillows, black and trimmed with golden lace, almost swallowed him. He tried to sit up to kiss her, but her hands pushed him back down.

"Lie back and relax." She ran her hands out over his chest, dragging her nails as she pulled them back to her. He moaned, so she repeated the act again and again. "Your muscles are so tight. Just let me work you for a bit." She let out a muted laugh. "Those farm girls of yours know nothing of the art of massage, do they?"

He shook his head and melted into the bed as she spent the next hour slowly massaging and teasing him. She watched his expression change as her hands rubbed him. Whatever reservations or nerves he may have had dissolved away. His eyes closed and his body responded to her every touch.

She climbed up and straddled the man, perfectly positioned to look down onto his purely innocent face. Taking him into her, she rode the man, careful not to overstimulate. She wanted it to last, not just for her pleasure, but to drive him insane, to break him completely.

The little death came to her many times over the course of the evening, but she denied it to him. The young man had far more stamina than she had imagined, but that only made the night better.

What was the English saying? 'The bigger they are, the harder they fall.

Mata could not help but laugh as she rolled her hips over and over, causing the man's eyes to roll back in his head. The skill of her movements brought him to a state of sexual bliss. She knew from his expression that he had lost perspective of the who's, where's and when's of the world. Nothing outside this chamber mattered. For him, only she meant anything, and he would give her whatever she desired to make their time together last a while longer.

"Please." He begged. "I need the release."

Shaking her head, she replied. "All in due time."

Reaching to the nightstand, she slowly tugged a pair of silk scarfs loose from one another. Taking one, she took his right wrist and pulled it to the headboard. In short order, the scarf bound him tightly to it.

"Wha—what are you doing?" Between deep breaths, the man spoke with a bit of panic in his tone.

Mata stopped for a moment, lightly brushed her fingertips along his cheek, and picked up the other scarf.

"General Gouraud must have mentioned that I am a skilled courtesan? Skilled in all the ways to bring the greatest amount of pleasure to men?" she said as she bound his left wrist.

Blushing, he replied with a slight nod. "The best in all the land. He's quite taken with you. As are others in the High Command."

Nodding, she let a small laugh escape her lips. The General came to her often and had been bewitched by her charms so completely that he confided more in her then he did to all the officers in the Army's General Staff combined.

"The General, my Henri, loves the feel of my silk against his wrists. He asked that I take special care of you, in the same ways that he and I play. Now, mon beau, tug at the knots and see if you can escape."

He tried and failed to gain his freedom. "I don't understand. This is…"

"Not what you are used to? I would think not. Young farm girls may have their charms, but they lack the knowledge of what men need, lack the skills to pleasure a man beyond words, or understand the forbidden ways in which men enjoy being teased and used." She moved off him and sat up on her knees, beside him, letting her hands caress his chest. "My

Henri and I play a special game. In all honesty, many officers desire this, so I suspect that you'll enjoy it more than you can imagine."

His eyes darted around but finally settled on Mata. He laid back and asked. "What kind of game?"

The corners of her lips twitched upwards. "Mon beau, in a time of war like this, officers are taught and trained to keep secrets. They teach you to fear being caught and interrogated by the cruel Krauts. You have knowledge that you're forbidden from sharing with those closest to you. Not family, friends, or lovers." She let a hand slowly move down his chest, inching further down as she spoke. "But some men find a unique enjoyment. Should we say a forbidden pleasure in having those secrets pulled from them by a woman of skill, such as myself."

His eyes widened. "The General has given you secrets?"

"All men surrender their secrets to me," she purred as her hand found him erect and ready for manipulation. "Don't fear, mon amour, I'm no more a spy than you are. But…" her nails brushed and lightly scrapped against his manhood. "It is the idea of the act, being broken and made to betray one's country that arouses men, men like your General, his officers…" Her hand snaked down a bit further, letting her fingers wrap around his testicles. With a gentle squeeze, she made her point. "And you, my pet."

Snatching a small bottle from the nightstand, she poured a small amount of the scented oil into her hands and then poured what remained onto his groin. Mata moved between his legs, sitting as her hands reached out, rubbing up his inner thighs until she had him within her grasp again.

"Tonight, you will be broken. Tonight, you will belong to me," she glared into his eyes as her hands began to work, faster and faster. "And tonight, you will surrender your mind, body, and secrets to your Goddess."

His body shook violently as pulses of ecstasy burrowed into his brain. Opening his eyes wide and staring into hers, the young officer struggled to speak.

"Who do you belong to, my pet?"

"You, Goddess. I belong to you."

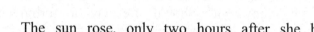

The sun rose, only two hours after she had allowed Archard to enjoy his little death. Mata should have been exhausted, but a night of passion always left her invigorated the next morning.

Sleep is for the old, the melancholy, and the dead, she thought, and rolled from the bed.

An hour later, she had bathed, dressed, and kissed the young Lieutenant as they stepped into the hallway.

"Archard, à bientôt and remember, Henri, I mean, the General does not discuss our relationship or what his preferences are. A slip of a tongue could cause great hardships to come to him or his family or his men. So, if he asks, tell him that you had the night of your life and keep the details of our little games to yourself. If you do, then I'll consider asking Henri if you can return."

His eyes lit up at the last part. "You have my word. I'll remain silent." He took her hand and bent to kiss it. "Please, let me return soon. I have no words that can express my feelings. That game, it was intoxicating. You were right, something about giving my secrets was strangely arousing."

Mata only smiled and stepped back into her apartment, knowing that he would be back with even more secrets for her to pluck from his weak mind.

"Portez-vous bien, mon'goddess," he said as he bowed and walked away.

Standing beside the window moments later, she watched as he left the building and strolled a short way down the road before calling for a cab. Satisfied he would not be returning she moved to her writing desk and carefully began to scribble notes. The words flowed from her, chronicling every detail she had drawn from her helpless prey. At the bottom of the third page, she drew a decorative M, her signature to those in the Kriegsnachrichtenstelle West.

An hour later, Mata went for her daily stroll, stopping only to deposit her writing. The pages had been folded and sealed in an envelope. She glanced around, stepped into an alley, and pulled a loose brick from its place on the wall of one of the buildings. After slipping the envelope inside, she replaced the brick and continued her walk to her favorite café.

"More, Madame?" the waiter asked.

She gave a nod and watched as steam rose from the torrent of coffee as he refilled her cup. Each morning, Mata found her way to Le Café Lis Rose for her breakfast, typically an egg, toast, and coffee. After a long night of seducing and working her prey, pumping him for information and enjoying herself in the process, she sorely needed the coffee to make it through the rest of the day.

A little cream and a dash of sugar were gingerly tossed in and stirred to take the edge off the bold flavor. The first cup, black and strong, had soured her stomach but she needed more. The first sip of the refilled cup passed over her lips and she sighed in contentment. Still waiting on the caffeine to kick in, she leaned back in her chair and watched the people walking past. After years of being in the bustling atmosphere of Paris, she never grew tired of watching them. So many styles, so many men to choose from.

Her eyes met another set that looked directly at her. They belonged to a well-built gentleman, smartly dressed in a tailored suit. She nonchalantly sipped her beverage as he approached and, without saying a word, took the chair opposite from her.

"Monsieur, some would consider it rude to take a chair without asking permission first." Her words purred across the table and only served to make the man smile.

"Madame, no offense was meant, but I couldn't help myself." He spoke French well enough, but his accent was British, and his stiff demeanor only served to confirm his nationality.

He waved to the waiter and asked for tea.

"Again, monsieur, you presume to order without knowing if I intend to entertain you?"

"I think you'll entertain...," he started, but a greasy-looking Frenchman stepped up, wearing a pin-striped suit, pushing a photo and a pen in front of Mata.

"Pardon Madame, but I attended your performance last night and failed to get an autograph

One Life for Another

from you. Would you mind?" Said the Frenchman.

Mata looked up at the man who held out a black and white promotional picture. Taking it, she glanced at the front and saw her own nearly nude image. Selling the artistic photos at her performances had been Oscar's idea, and a good one, considering the number they sold. Placing it on the table, backside up, she gave him a smile and held out a hand for the pen.

Quickly, she scribbled some words, along with her name. Finally, she added two small hearts to the signature.

Handing it back, she said in a seductive tone, "Merci for attending last night. I do hope to see you again at my next performance."

Nodding his thanks, the Frenchman turned and quickly disappeared into the crowded sidewalk. Mata watched him go for a moment before returning her gaze on the British man, sitting across from her.

"Are you still here?" she asked, playfully moving her fingers along the sides of her coffee cup.

"I am," he replied and then looked to a spot above and to the right of her. Raising his hand, he lifted two fingers. When his eyes returned to hers, she tilted her head slightly, silently questioning his behavior. "Come now, Miss Hari. Or would you prefer Mata?"

Curious, she glanced over her shoulder, trying to see what had his interest. On the third floor of the apartment building across the street, sat an elderly woman on a balcony, waving a red scarf.

"The color red stands for two," he said, and she turned her gaze back to him. "Two hearts."

Raising an eyebrow and feigning ignorance, she said, "Two hearts? I always add a heart or two to my signatures."

"I know, or should I say, we know." He replied

19

and reached for his tea, as the waiter approached. Glancing up at the man, he added, "Thank you. This looks lovely but could you fetch a lemon wedge? I do like mine tart."

"Tart? You English and your tea." She said, watching the waiter scamper off. "May I ask your name and the reason my signature interests you so much?"

Sipping the tea first, he relaxed for the first time and eyed her. Speaking in a hushed manner, he began answering her question. "Interest me? Well, shall we start with the young man you entertained last night, or more to the point, the military officer you invited to your performance, lured into your chambers, and then seduced, I would assume, into spilling all manner of classified secrets? Those secrets were written down this morning, left in a secret location, a dead drop, I believe they are called by those in the trade, and then left for your German spymaster to collect."

With an elbow on the table and her hand under her chin, she smiled and appraised the Brit. "If you know me, then you know of my weakness for beautiful men. That officer was my guest at the performance, as are many of the officers of the High Command."

"Ahhh, yes. Your weakness. Funny that your weakness only applies to men who are in positions of power or work for those in power, so that they are privy to military secrets." He stopped talking as the waiter approached with a lemon wedge on a plate. Holding the cup out, he said in a loud voice, "Just drop it in, please."

Mata glanced back to the old woman, who was now watching her. Before she could say anything, the Brit spoke.

"Now. Once I finish my tea, we'll head back to your apartment, pack a bag for a two-week journey across the Channel, where you'll meet with my superior."

Her eyes opened wide in surprise. "Oh, will I? And what makes you think…" Her words trailed off as two men moved up behind the Brit, staring at her.

"Madame, you can come with me or," he paused for effect and then leaned closer to her, "as an ally of France, it'll be our duty to arrest you and turn you over to the authorities. We have sources in the Parisian newspapers and ample evidence of your treachery. You're spying for the Krauts. Even your precious General Gouraud would be unable to protect you, once public opinion has tainted your reputation." Mata began to say something, but he spoke again before her words could take form. "And should you escape, where would you go? Germany? You'd have allies there, but only for a short time. We have friendly folks in Berlin who'd love to spread word of your spying for the French. This war has most of the world divided into two factions, you see, so either side you run to will have plenty of reason to despise you and think of you as nothing more than a traitorous whore."

"I am no whore," she said in a venomous tone, leaning forward. "The men who come to me do shower me with gifts in appreciation for the nights of love they share with me. They provide for me, not out of payment or request, but because I can be the woman, any woman, they desire."

The Brit smiled, then cleared his throat. "Perhaps that wasn't the most appropriate word. Would 'courtesan' work better?"

She settled back in her chair, took a deep breath,

and weighed her options.

"What do you English want with me?" A devilish grin appeared on her face. "Am I to provide comfort to someone of importance? You know, I have admirers in the British ranks as well." When she saw no give in his expression she added, "Perhaps I'll get to see John French again.' Mata smiled as his eyebrows rose slightly. "Were you unaware? You see, your lovable, yet stuffy Field Marshal and I have spent many wonderful nights embracing as lovers."

He gave a slow nod. "You'll be well taken care of, but no our Field Marshal will not be seeing you on this journey." He pulled a pack of cigarettes from his shirt pocket, plucked one out, then offered her one.

"A proper lady doesn't smoke in public. And I don't recall you mentioning your name," she purred.

"Edward Black." The Brit tilted his head and smiled as he extended his hand again with the pack, "A proper lady doesn't smoke in public? So why would that stop you?"

"How rude!" Smacking her lips in feigned annoyance, she took one and allowed the man to light it for her. Blowing the first puff of smoke out, she had a thought which made her worry.

"You mentioned the hearts earlier. Why?"

"Because Madame, we are aware that your spymaster has several dead drops. Each one numbered. You leave your secrets, written down on expensive, albeit easily obtained stationary at one of the drops, and then take a short stroll here for a leisurely breakfast. An agent always asks for an autograph, pretending to be an admirer, who you always oblige. The number of hearts on the signature signifies which dead drop you used. Then he scurries off, collects your notes, and forwards them to your

German spymaster, who gets the information to Germany." His expression changed slightly, and she realized that he saw the worried expression she wore. "Not to fear, Madame. Your messenger will be unmolested. He'll collect this morning's message and pass it along, just as he always does. Your spymaster will make the usual deposit into your bank account, so you still get paid for last night's work, if that's what you call it."

Reluctantly, she asked, "If you know all of this, why not shut down the entire spy ring?"

"Because, for the past month, every message in each dead drop has been replaced with another one that we've concocted. Your penmanship along with those of four other spies in Paris have been studied and duplicated by our staff. The German High Command is getting just enough real information to make everything look genuine, but every message is leading their armies into a trap."

"Again, I'll ask. Why do you need me?"

He stood and reached out a hand to help her to her feet. "Because Madame, your skills may be the very thing that will save Germany and the rest of the continent when the war ends."

D. Alan Lewis

One Life for Another

Part Two: Unknown Lands

"Welcome to Bletchley Hall," Mr. Black said.

Standing in front of the manor house, Mata felt dwarfed by its size. The place was expansive and impressively beautiful. Giving a slight nod, she approved. It was not what she expected at all after making the overnight journey from Paris.

The trip had consisted of a mad dash across the French countryside by train to the port city of Bordeaux. From there, a fast-civilian cutter, flying a Danish flag, took Mata and Mr. Black to Penzance, where another train awaited.

"I'm sure you'll sleep better here," Mr. Black said as he moved up behind her, carrying her twin bags.

Through bloodshot eyes, she glared at him. "An overnight ride on that sorry excuse of a train didn't help. I fail to see why we're in such a rush. A night's sleep in Penzance surely wouldn't have disrupted any military timetables or any such nonsense."

"My orders are to deliver you here this morning." He dropped the bags and pulled out a pocket watch. "Excellent. We're an hour ahead of schedule. Perhaps a quick lunch can be whipped up before we meet with the Admiral."

"And will he be able to tell me why I've been brought to your wretched island?" Mata huffed. Her anger had steadily risen throughout the trip. Mr. Black refused to give her any details about the journey or the purpose for bringing her to a remote estate in northern England. Furthermore, every attempt to use her skills to sway the young man had been met with cold stares and tight lips.

"The Admiral? He is the reason you've been

25

brought here. And the British Isles are not wretched. We're merely drained, expended, and tired, due to constant fighting to defend our allies and keep Paris out of the Kaiser's grasp."

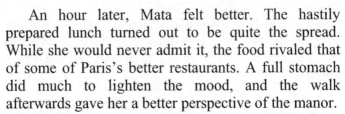

An hour later, Mata felt better. The hastily prepared lunch turned out to be quite the spread. While she would never admit it, the food rivaled that of some of Paris's better restaurants. A full stomach did much to lighten the mood, and the walk afterwards gave her a better perspective of the manor.

"Here we are." Mr. Black swung the double doors open to the opulent office of Admiral Thomas Ellison.

Like the rest of the manor, the office felt almost too big for a single man to use. The Victorian Gothic styling of the estate had, over the years, been mixed with touches of Tudor and Dutch Baroque, making it a unique and stylish sight.

Mr. Black waved her through the door. "After you, Madame." Approaching the large oak desk, he cleared his throat to gain the attention of the balding man who sat behind it, busily writing. "Admiral Ellison, may I present Madame Mata Hari."

The officer reached for a smoldering pipe that lay in a tray on the right side of the desk and looked up at her as he took it between his lips. Giving a quick puff, he nodded and pointed to a chair beside her.

"Thank you, Black. That'll be all," he said and watched the younger man exit the room before returning his gaze to Mata. "No doubt you have questions."

One Life for Another

"You have me at a disadvantage. I have no idea why I'm here." She let a tinge of anger seep into her tone.

"We've known about your activities for some time now, Miss Hari." He pulled a thick and battered file folder from a desk drawer, and slowly flipped it open. Adjusting his glasses, he ignored her stare and turned page after page until she finally cleared her throat in frustration.

"Do you intend to keep me waiting all day in this dank, oversized hellhole?"

"Mata Hari, originally known as Margaretha Geertuida Zelle. You were born in Leeuwarden. Married and lived in the Dutch East Indies for several years. You've been in Paris for the past few years, but you've retained your Dutch citizenship. Thus, with Dutch neutrality in the current conflict, you have the freedom to move about the continent even during wartime, since you supposedly hold no allegiance to any of the warring parties." He glanced up and smiled. "The perfect advantage for a spy during these troubled times, don't you think?"

Looking annoyed, she just leaned back and huffed at the statement. She quickly sized the man up. The gold band on his ring finger held no shine, meaning that he never took it off, something that cheating husbands tend to do. His unkempt hair and the awkward angle his tie hung suggested that he was not living with his wife, although that may have been for any number of reasons. His reluctance to look her in the eyes or even study her in any way indicated that he either enjoyed the company of lovely women often and didn't want to be charmed by her appearance or he'd been away from his wife for longer than a man should be parted from his love.

27

"Married only once to a Dutch Army Captain, but your time with him was not a happy one. Mother of two but one child died during your time in the -"

"That is really enough." Mata let her anger boil out as she interrupted the Admiral. "I have no need to have my life splayed out for your examination."

He paused and flipped another page, ignoring her frustrations. "It seems your husband indulged too much in his drink. The kind of indulging that leads to unhappy and abusive relationships. I've seen that sort of thing all too often." He flipped another page and continued. "And then you left him and moved to Paris to find fame and fortune as an exotic dancer and self-proclaimed expert on all things Asian."

"Self-proclaimed?" She started to get up, but he gave a slow shake of his head. "My knowledge of the mysteries of the Orient is well-known and appreciated by those in the Parisian upper classes. Now, enough of the polite chit-chat, as you Brits say. What do you want?"

He closed the folder and turned his gaze to her. "The war is going well for us. The Allies will obtain victory within the next year or so, and preparations have begun in planning the state of Europe as well as the world when peace takes root. German colonies will be claimed by the victors, and that'll no doubt stir up a bit of squabbling. Better to get things like that sorted out in advance."

"And what does that have to do with me?"

Admiral Ellison puffed again on his pipe and squinted at her through the smoke. "A particular general in the German Army has been talking about waging a new and somewhat disturbing form of war after a cease of hostilities."

She laughed, interrupting him. "If hostilities have

ceased, then there is no longer a need to battle on."

"Yes, well, while I'd agree with you on that, I don't think you understand his meaning and future plans. While the Allies may occupy the Fatherland in the end, he means to issue commands to his armies to disband and flock to the hills, so as to wage a guerrilla war of resistance, keeping the German people in a state of continual chaos for years, perhaps decades. Any conquered nation can heal in time, but only if all parties have stopped the fighting and work together toward living in harmony and peace. This man has no desire for peace of any kind. From what we know, he is the force that urged…, no, pushed the Kaiser into this militaristic mindset during his youth, and some say he twisted young Wilhelm's arm to get him to declare war at the onset of this nightmare."

"I doubt that, but again, why does this require my presence here?"

"We've gotten word that he's laying out the groundwork for such a plan, preparing caches of weapons and supplies throughout the German countryside. Imagine, Miss Hari, the effects, not just on Germany but on the whole of Europe. For that matter, with Europe kept in a state of constant flux, all of the colonies throughout the world will feel the turmoil, as will the United States in time. Even your beloved homeland will suffer, drained of resources as the center of Europe will draw in all those nations around it in order to survive a prolonged state of warfare."

He paused briefly and considered his words. "When the war started, no one thought it would last more than a few months. It's been years now and look at the world. His Majesty's Government has borrowed so much from the Americans in cash and supplies that I doubt we'll ever be able to repay it. With the constant strain on people and resources in Russia, the people are on the verge of revolt. I doubt Nicholas and his government will last another year. And you've seen France. Outside of the posh neighborhoods of Paris, the place is a shell-shocked hobble of people and half-burnt-out villages, grasping onto the hope that the smoke will clear, and all will magically return to the halcyon days before the war."

Mata pursed her lips and thought about it before speaking. "I believe in the resiliency of the French people. They'll restore everything quickly. Their pride is too strong to allow them to wallow in misery."

"No, Ms Hari, I fear they won't. It'll never be the same. Not for a long while."

She leaned forward, resting an elbow on the edge of his desk, and propping her head in her hand. "And I'm no warrior, but even if your madman attempts what you say, his men will never follow orders of that kind."

"That is wishful thinking, my dear. Some can't handle defeat and will gladly fight on. A guerrilla war in Germany will not be confined to just the Rhine, but like a cancer, it will grow and consume everything in time."

Ellison smiled and pointed his pipe at her. "We need a surgeon to probe our patient, the German High Command, and excise the cancerous seed before it takes root."

Mata glared at him, a sinking feeling growing in her stomach. "Are you suggesting that I am to be the surgeon?" He gave a slow nod and she responded calmly, but barely containing her anger at the absurdity of the notion. "Admiral, I am a dancer, a lover to many men, and yes, a spy. I am, unfortunately for you, not an assassin. Killing is not in my nature. It is a barbaric practice which I have neither the desire nor the need to attempt."

"We plan on instilling that killing nature within you. Before you leave Bletchley Park, you'll be our little rock that will slay the mighty Goliath. You'll be trained in a variety of techniques before you go. Hand to hand, firearms, and improvised weaponry, to name a few."

Mata scoffed at the notion. "You presume to tell me what I will do? You expect me to allow myself to be perverted into a killer for you and your King. Nothing more than a criminal with a gun? What makes you think I'll do this?"

"Black should have mentioned that you have no real option. We can hand you over to the French as a spy, or you can run to the Germans for shelter where they'll hang you for being a double agent. You can try the Americas. Let's assume you escape here. The United States would be your only true option, but, as a spy, the Allies will place a bounty on your head so large that every bounty hunter in the Colonies will be after you. And given their cowboy attitudes, you wouldn't last long or live to stand trial." Ellison looked her over and smiled like the Devil. "Now, will you work on behalf of His Majesty's Government or…?"

Mata considered her options. They had her beat, there was no doubt. Internally, she cursed herself. Where had she failed? How had she slipped up and let the Brits catch on to her love of espionage, the thrill and danger of it all?

No, she thought.

There would be time to retrace her actions later

and learn from her mistakes. Now, the man across the desk needed an answer and there was only one to give. But she would make the most of this, one way or another.

"Black did mention that you knew of my activities. The man didn't say much more, no matter how hard I tried," Mata said.

Ellison furrowed his brow. "You tried?"

She scoffed, "I tried, but the man is obviously a homosexual. It seems he is immune to my charms, resisted every attempt to touch or draw him in close, and never once took the opportunity to gaze upon the wonders of my body. Much the way your eyes have not strayed from their examination of my cleavage for the past few minutes."

His gaze immediately moved upward to meet hers. "You were undressed in his presence?"

"Admiral, knowing that I enjoy the company of men, especially young attractive men, would you expect me not to try and lure him into my confidence? Yet nothing from him. Not one nod of interest. Not one show of arousal or embarrassment. So he confirmed my suspicions. He prefers members of his own sex. Knowing that your government despises men of that type, I assume you'll have him drummed out of your service and imprisoned?"

Ellison smiled, "Not at all. The young man is married to my daughter. Since knowing of your capabilities to bend the wills of men, I decided to send someone I could trust - after all, if he gave into your temptations, you'd immediately brag about it upon arriving. Knowing your reputation, you seem to enjoy letting superiors know when you've defiled or broken their men. It is a particular thrill of yours. Oh, you're not reckless with that information. You brag only to the right men, who enjoy hearing of your exploits. You'd have told me if he strayed and he knew this too, serving to reinforce his resolve."

Mata narrowed her eyes and nodded. "Well-played, Admiral."

He gave a curt nod. "Now, Mr. Black will show you to your room. After you've had some time to unpack and rest, we'll introduce you to Major Perkins. He's our expert on women's hand-to-hand combat techniques, as well as other tactics of subduing and eliminating an opponent. You'll be training with him. Then two hours of briefing on your target and what we've learned about his schedule for the target date. And after that, other courses."

Mata cleared her throat before she spoke. "I will require no less than two hours each morning to dance and exercise." She noticed Ellison's sour expression. "I am a dancer, a performer, and I need constant practice to keep my skills sharp and my body toned."

"Very well, your needs should pose no difficulty." He paused for a moment and cleared his throat. "I will insist that the practicing of your skills be limited to just your dance and performance techniques. Your sexual appetites are to be set aside during your time here. Training and preparation for the mission are to take precedence over anything else. Do I make myself clear?"

"Again, I must practice all of my skills," Mata said.

Turning a few pages in the folder, Ellison spent a few seconds reading before looking up at her.

"While in the East Indies, we know you studied with a Javanese mystic who'd taught you the ways of relaxing the minds of others."

Mata shifted uncomfortably in her seat. "Yes.

That's true."

"After returning to Europe, you learned this practice was remarkably close to hypnosis. Sources tell us you delved deeply into the study of it and combined the two into a powerful process for bewitching the minds of the weak."

Mata smiled and relaxed somewhat. "As I said, my skills require practice."

"You can go a while without practicing THAT one." Ellison said in a stern voice.

"Well, if you insist. Although I'm sure you know where my room is. Feel free to visit, if…"

He held up a hand to stop her. Smiling, she nodded and then they both stood. Noticing his attention had moved to something behind her, she turned to see Mr. Black entering the office.

"Black will be on hand to take care of any needs that may arise during your stay. I am pleased that you've decided to help. This isn't about King and Country. This about preventing the coming Armageddon."

Mata started to speak but hesitated. From the description of the German general, she had an idea of who it was, but she hoped her guess was incorrect. Still, she needed to know.

"Before I go, there is one thing you've failed to tell me. Who is the target you speak of?"

Ellison's voice came out cold and lacked emotion, "General Otto Kripker of the Western Army. From your expression, I see you know him. Knowing his strengths, you can understand our fears."

She knew Kripker intimately and nothing they were saying made sense. They spoke of a madman, not the kind-hearted German she had known during better times, times before the war.

For the next two weeks, Mata reluctantly began her days at dawn. She easily handled the morning exercise routines and thoroughly enjoyed out-shining Jennifer; the young woman charged with ensuring her physical fitness. No one could deny that her strength, flexibility, and reflexes were beyond reproach.

Exercise and dance were followed by a generous breakfast. The meal tugged at her heart, making her miss her little café's eggs, toast, and coffee.

Mission briefings followed breakfast. Two hours of talks regarding her target and other items of importance. She liked this part of her day the least. She found herself purposely lingering at the breakfast table.

"How many times must I tell you, I know the man? Other than a few details about his current activities due to the war, I know more about his moods and tastes…"

Andrew Barber glared at her with barely contained rage and disgust each time she complained. She despised the little man and knew the feeling was mutual. He was the epitome of everything she hated about the British - stuffy, arrogant, and bent on world domination. Mata really could not tell if he hated all women or just her in particular, but he never failed to express his feelings whenever opportunity arose.

"Tastes? Yes, I'm sure you'd know all about his tastes, just as every whore in the Rhineland does." He seemed impervious to her glares. If other men saw her expression, they would retreat in fear, but not Mr.

Barber. "Kripker is a notorious womanizer, bedding down with whatever courtesan, prostitute, or street tramp he can get his claws in. Did you know it's rumored that he has a couple of French girls, supposedly captured during his time in the Ardennes? Seems they have been forcibly recruited as slave labor, working as his personal maids. But they say he uses them for other darkly deviant purposes too."

"I wouldn't know about that." Mata smiled and let her wicked tongue lash the man with her words. "When he has been with me, there was never a need for any other woman to be about. But I'm sure you wouldn't understand how a woman can so satisfy a man. Tell me, Mr. Barber. Do you enjoy the company of women? The way you speak of the man, always mentioning his appetites, should we say? It makes one wonder if you don't fancy the man yourself. Perhaps you prefer the masculine to the feminine?"

He cleared his throat, staring daggers at her, which amused her greatly. "You don't have a clue as to how dangerous the man is, do you? If allowed to succeed after Germany collapses, the result could be..."

"Yes, yes. That's what you all keep saying. This man you describe is far different from the man I know."

Barber sighed. "I'm aware of that. You mentioned yesterday that you've not seen him since the war began. Our records show him to have been a reasonable officer before hostilities began. But since the fighting began, it seems his passion for victory will no longer allow him to consider defeat or any form of a peace accord between our peoples."

"You paint him as a monster. I can't accept that," she replied.

Barber smirked as he leaned closer over the table toward her. "You say you know the man, so tell me about him."

Mata hesitated, uncertain of what game Barber was playing. "You know all about him."

"No, no. Please enlighten me. I know only the facts that were known before the war and what our intelligence has determined over the past couple of years. Tell me the details that only a whor..." He paused and reconsidered the word. "...a woman such as yourself would have learned from your times with him." They stared at one another for a moment before he spoke again. "Or didn't you pump him for information like all those other men before and since?"

Mata's right hand squeezed the pencil she held so tight that it snapped in two. She narrowed her eyes at him, furious at the slight grin that was slowly growing on his wrinkled face.

"I'm not a killer, but they tell me that after my training here, I'll be adept at it." She smiled, opened her hand, and dropped the wood shards to the table. "I know men like you - bureaucrats and pencil-pushers. After this mission is done with, I may put these new skills to some use. I'll find some means of murdering you, preferably in some emasculating method."

His curt laugh did nothing to help the tension. "Now, if we can only direct that passion for killing in the right direction, we may have the perfect weapon against him."

And with that said, the briefing continued the way it usually did, with both sides frustrated.

The last thirty minutes of the briefings took a different route. Barber interrogated her about the information she had learned during her nights working as a spy, and what information she had passed on to both sides. During this time, a pair of clerks joined them, each taking furious notes of her tales.

Bonnie, a young redhead who spoke with a soft and endearing Irish accent, usually kept her head down, but occasionally lifted her gaze to Mata, eyeing her in a longing manner. Her cohort Joseph, a young Welshman with curly black hair, occasionally incurred the wrath of Mr. Barber by being bold enough to ask for clarification on her answers or to ask a few of his own. After the first week of interrogations, the topic of British troop and naval movements in the Dardanelles arose.

"I think I may have cost that nice chap Churchill his job on that one," Mata mused. She did not hesitate when she saw their questioning looks. "Before the, what do you call them? Naval landings? Yes, before those landings, I entertained several British officers and members of the Chief of Staff, including Sir Hamilton. They all, especially dear Ian, gave me the details of the operations and landings, all the way down to which beaches they planned on occupying first." The room went as silent as a tomb and Mata knew she had hit a nerve. "Well, as usual, the information was passed on to my messengers and from there to Berlin. Given your lack of success there, I take it they put my messages to good use."

Mata watched as Barber stubbed out a cigarette, leaving the smoldering butt behind as he stood and quietly left the room. The tension grew thicker until the pencil Joseph held snapped between his fingers. Like Barber, he stood and left.

Bonnie watched him leave and then spoke up as

she also stood to follow the men from the room. Her words came out slow and thick with sadness. "You'll have to forgive them. That defeat hurt a lot of us, in different ways. Many of us had friends or loved ones who fell on those damned shores."

The fighting and weapons training came after lunch. While the Brits could cook up a passable breakfast, their ideas for lunchtime foods tended to sour her stomach as much as the time spent with Mr. Barber.

Although she had always abhorred guns, Mata found that firing them was not as bad as she'd first thought. The reports of each shot stung her ears at first, but once training really began, Gerald Jackson, who resembled a scarecrow more than a man, provided her with earmuffs. With the noise diminished, target practice became something of a joy, a dangerous albeit provocative sport. If it were not for the killing aspect of the weaponry she trained with, Mata thought she could see herself taking up target shooting as a future pastime.

Jackson watched as she unloaded the revolver, firing each shot into the chest of the paper silhouette, fifty feet down-range. Just as he had taught her, Mata stood, feet apart, and arms extended but relaxed to absorb the weapon's kick.

"Excellent, Ms Hari. A crack shot with only a couple of weeks' worth of practice. But in the field, one doesn't always have the option of standing in the correct firing posture at an unmoving target. Now, reload quickly and we'll try something new," he said, and moved closer to her as she dumped out the weapon's spent shells and placed fresh bullets in their place. Grasping her upper arms, he turned her partially around so that the target was to her right. Taking her left hand into his, he stepped back and nodded to the target. "Again, but one shot at a time."

The gun was brought up and she took aim but as her finger pulled the trigger, he yanked her arm. The bullet flew wide and missed the hanging paper completely.

She glanced back at him. "What was the purpose…" Her words trailed off, and then she whispered the answer. "Because in combat, I might be moving, and so would the target."

"Correct, Miss Hari. But something else to consider is that you may be on a moving vehicle when you need to take a shot. You have to learn to anticipate the target's movements, your movements, and the possibility of being in a bouncing automobile or a train."

She scoffed. "It's impossible to be accurate with all those difficulties stacked against you."

He nodded back to the target. "That is why we practice, so that we can *make* the impossible shot. Do you remember our discussion about leading your target when they're moving? Same principle applies here. Now, raise your weapon, anticipate your possible movements, and try again."

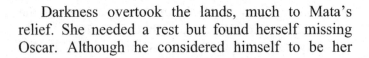

Darkness overtook the lands, much to Mata's relief. She needed a rest but found herself missing Oscar. Although he considered himself to be her manager and agent, the man worshipped and served her as a slave would his queen. Turning the faucets, she marveled at how easy it was to draw a hot bath. In her Parisian home, Oscar would toil for an hour to heat enough water on the stove for a proper bath.

She untied her robe, and almost had it slipped over her shoulders when she heard a light knock at the door. The staff typically knocked loud and repeatedly, but this was soft, almost timid. A smile appeared as she pulled the robe together and tied it shut. Only the light from her bathroom illuminated the main room of her quarters, making the crack at the bottom of the door appear as a glowing bar, punctuated by a pair of shadows. Mata watched the shadows of the knocker's feet bouncing and stepping to and fro. They were small and delicate, just as the knocking had been.

A woman, Mata thought. *A nervous woman, who's sneaking around at night to see me. Might this be my lovely Bonnie?*

Opening the door, she saw green eyes, set in a pale and freckled face, framed by flowing waves of red hair. The woman's eyes were wide open, and her rich full lips were frozen in mid-word. She shook slightly from fear or nerves, something that Mata had become accustomed to, over her years.

Knowing that an opportunity existed here, she decided to use it to her advantage. As she spoke, Mata let loose the full force of her sexuality upon the unsuspecting young woman.

"Bonjour, Bonnie. What has you in such a nerveux state ce soir? Please, come in and sit with me. It's been a while since I've had a la demoiselle to converse with."

Looking both ways before moving, Bonnie

stepped across the threshold. "Thank you. I'm not really sure…"

Mata closed and locked the door, then turned and stepped close to her. Raising a hand, she brushed the stray hairs from Bonnie's face, letting her head tip to the side as she studied the young woman. Mata had spent time with Bonnie each day since arriving, yet the dim lights brought out a beauty that she had overlooked in the clerk.

"Please, sit with me and we can talk about why you're here."

She motioned to a pair of chairs and Bonnie moved to take a seat but hesitated until Mata had sat.

A very submissive act, Mata thought. S*o many possibilities here.*

But then a moment of doubt entered her head. Bonnie showing up and acting this way? Could this be some sort of trick? A trap, testing whether she would keep her word about seducing any of the Admiral's staff?

Why should I let any of that nonsense bother me? I am Mata Hari. She came here of her own free will. If she breaks, all the better. If not, at least I'll get some entertainment this evening.

"I'm sorry for interrupting. I hope I didn't wake you," Bonnie whispered.

As she crossed her legs in a slow and deliberate move, Mata replied, "Wake? No, no. I'd just drawn a bath." She sighed, "The wonders of wealth. I'm really quite envious of this manor. Hot water at the twist of a knob. Remarkable."

Bonnie smiled and let out a small laugh. "It is wonderful, isn't it? I grew up a few miles from here. I don't think I had had a decent bath, let alone a hot one, until I was recruited to the service."

Scooting up in the seat, Mata leaned closer to her. She reached out and ran her fingers along the woman's cheek. "What is it that brought you to me this evening?"

Bonnie's face flushed and she shyly turned away, but Mata's fingers tugged gently under her chin and brought the woman's head around. Their eyes locked, and Mata caressed the shy woman again as she repeated the question.

Reluctantly, Bonnie said, "I want to be like you. A real spy, living in Paris and doing my part in the war effort."

"I know that you wish to help your nation, but is that all you seek? I think you desire the power, the power of seduction. The ability to claim a man's heart as your property and use it in any manner you wish." Mata watched Bonnie's head nod in agreement. "I was a shy one myself, many years ago. Like you, I wanted more, and had to learn what was necessary to become what I am today."

"Please teach me. I'll do anything to learn your secrets," Bonnie pleaded. She reached out and took Mata's hand. "I've been listening for days to your stories, your adventures. I've read everything, all the files that we have on you. They say you can bewitch the mind, seduce anyone, and get anything. Please..."

Mata feigned disinterest. In a practiced move, she tried to pull her hand away yet held tight, pulling Bonnie forward until the young woman slipped from her chair and fell to her knees. Letting go, Mata ran a hand along her cheek and let her fingers slip into her red locks. Her nails dragged across Bonnie's scalp and the woman's eyes closed in unabashed ecstasy.

"Relax, ma fille, just let my words fill your thoughts. Feel my fingers as they move, back and forth, back and forth." Mata said and continued the entrancement.

"Bonnie, relax and look at me. Look into my eyes and see your reflection. Breathe slowly and look at yourself. Look into my eyes and see your own and relax. Your need for power comes from a place of weakness. You must embrace that submissive need if you are to ever have power. Embrace it and give it a name. A name for who holds your submission. Look and tell me who you see?"

Bonnie's eyelids fluttered. In a whisper she spoke. "I see myself in your eyes."

Mata's fingers lightened their movements. "Good lass. You see yourself within me?"

"Yes," Bonnie whispered.

"What you are seeing is your mind's way of explaining the truth of the matter. Without me, there is no you that you're seeing in the reflection, correct?"

Bonnie looked confused for a moment before answering. "Yes."

"Without me there is no you that you can see, correct?"

Bonnie's eyes glazed over, and she slowly shook her head. "Yes."

"That's right, mon cheri. Without me, you don't exist. To be what you desire, you must accept that I am your universe. I am your everything. And you are mine. You are the clay that I will shape into what you desire most. But that process is long and means I will shape you in many ways that you don't expect. To get there, you must accept the new changes, the new shapes my hands mold you into being."

For thirty minutes, she spoke to the entranced woman, caressing Bonnie's mind into accepting her new position as Mata's pet. Something about the power, the ability to reshape someone's mind, thrilled and excited her in unspeakable ways. Mata leaned down and gently brushed her lips against her thrall. Her action drew a small moan from the woman and Mata continued. Lips brushed, caressed one another, and finally came together in a passionate kiss.

Pulling away, she looked down at the woman, who swooned and nearly fell to the side. Smiling, Mata stood. "Now awaken, my pet, and look upon your Mistress."

As if awakening from a deep slumber, Bonnie's eyes fluttered. She looked up at the goddess she knelt before. Her mind tried to make sense of what had happened. Mata loved watching this part, watching as the subjects found their realities remade into whatever image she deemed best for them, or more to the point, what was best for her. Bonnie remained in her kneeling position, eyes never leaving the splendid form of her new Mistress.

"If you've read everything known about me, then you know that I was not always the woman that I am today. In my youth, I was a slave to my husband's needs. One cannot be a goddess without knowing what it is to be a servant. Every General or Admiral, no matter how high, began as a lowly conscript." Mata reached down, taking the girl's hair in her hand and pulling it tight. She judged the pull was enough to get her point across without hurting the woman. "If you are to learn my secrets, you must first prove that you can serve. To have men kneel before you, you must be willing to kneel before your superior. You must know and gladly accept your role as a servant to your betters."

"Whatever you wish," Bonnie replied.

Mata's hand gently touched Bonnie's lips and let the woman kiss her fingertips.

"I'll... I'll do anything, please."

Knowing that she had the woman under her thumb, Mata looked into Bonnie's eyes as she untied and then slipped the robe over her shoulders, letting it fall to the floor. The young woman's eyes glanced up and down, taking in the view before returning to Mata's gaze.

"I've drawn a bath. Come, my pet, and bathe me."

For five more days, Mata's training routine continued unabated. Despite the uniformity of each day, she found that Barber and his clerk, Joseph, treated her with more and more disdain. Their stares and sharp, spiteful tones unnerved her, making her reluctant to divulge any new information. While she had always dealt with people looking down their noses at her and her profession, Mata had always been able to overcome any ill feeling in others through her conquests. But here, that form of relief had been forbidden. Only Bonnie gave her any joy.

Joseph's mood seemed especially dark around her. The young man stared at her with barely contained rage. Her skills at reading people sometimes felt more like a curse when she saw not just disapproval but sheer hatred in his eyes.

Bonnie, on the other hand, came to Mata every night and each time, she fell to her knees, allowing herself to be hypnotized, and let her mind accept her Mistress's words. Mata found it took little coaxing to turn her new pet into a skilled lover. The redhead found her place between her Mistress's thighs for hours at a time, worshipping at her temple.

Barber continued with his briefings, attempting to fill her head with useless trivia about Kripker. She listened but mostly ignored what was said.

"Ms Hari, I feel like I'm wasting my time. Your mind seems to be in another world whenever I discuss the General. You claim to know the man yet give me nothing when I ask your opinions. Our intelligence deems him to be a twisted individual, a madman who's been perverted by the power of his position."

Mata's mind had been elsewhere, namely thinking about her quarters and how much she would love to be there, with Bonnie.

"Mr. Barber," she started, but sighed from exhaustion and frustration. She was so tired of the daily routine. "I knew Otto long before the war began. He travelled to Paris often and I to Berlin. We spent many wonderful nights, entwined as lovers. But just before hostilities broke out in Serbia, something in him changed. Looking back, I think he saw the future, the war to come, and knew it was going to be his time to shine. He wasn't a man who longed for war, for combat, to test himself. He knew his worth without the need to prove it. I met with him in Munich during a visit, just after the Archduke had been murdered. He was not himself. He told me that if the war was over quickly, as everyone thought, he'd retire from the service. If it lasted longer, he told me to escape the hell the continent would become."

Barber studied her for a moment before asking, "I'm not certain I understand? Your tone implies he feared a prolonged war? Yet, our sources within Berlin are suggesting that he is the one who has been pushing the Kaiser to turn away our peace envoys, that he wishes to fight until the end, that he plans a campaign of terror and unrest when Germany falls." He paused and took a long draw on his cigarette. "You may be good at reading people, Ms Hari, but so am I and I can see you have feelings for the man. Perhaps you are not the one who should have been asked to perform this mission. Pulling the trigger on someone you care so deeply about would no doubt be difficult for you, and we can't risk having your personal emotions prevent you from completing the task we're training you for."

Mata leaned back in her chair. Taking a deep breath, she thought of how to respond. She did not want to kill her dear Otto, but if the war had changed him, driven him mad or altered his perception of reality, she more than anyone would have the best chance of killing him.

"He was a man to whom at one time, I could have given my heart. Every woman has that silly little girl deep inside her who can so deeply love a man and not care if he returns it." She gave a curt laugh. "That little girl in me died many years ago, but if she were to live on, her eyes would be fixed on Otto. I've enjoyed him in the past, and know I'll never have anything more than the memories of our nights together. I never feared him, and I don't think I ever will, despite what you may claim he has turned into." She cleared her throat and continued. "If he is now the man you claim, he should die before he unleashes his wretched plans."

The two sat a long while, not saying a word as they considered the conversation. Finally, Barber broke the silence.

"Miss Hari, I don't see that there is anything else I can tell you. Moving forward, let's concentrate on your physical and combat training." He paused and then softly added, "I... I am truly sorry that you've been put in this position. It isn't fair, but..."

She looked up and into his eyes and gave a curt nod. "It is necessary."

With her fighting and weapons training over for the day, she moved on to the last hour of the usual routine. She enjoyed this one as well. While there was still some sunlight left, her instructors worked on a daily rotation of equestrian riding, driving automobiles, and general techniques of moving on foot about the countryside while maintaining high levels of stealth.

"Mata, go ahead and ride up to the stables. I need to get back to the main house for a chat with the Admiral before he leaves for London."

The horse master, a middle-aged Scotsman named McDougal, had taken an immediate liking to Mata and so far, was the only member of Bletchley Park that called her by her first name. She did not get to see him daily, which saddened her, but he always brightened things up for her when she got to ride.

"Tell the boys up there that you put ol' Bessie through her paces today, and to make sure she is well taken care of."

He slapped the horse's hindquarters and walked off as Bessie began a leisurely trot up the winding dirty path to the stables. Mata enjoyed the feel of the horse beneath her. As a child, her father had taken her riding on many occasions. Those were some of the few happy memories of the Netherlands, before her father died and she was alone, left to fend for herself.

"Bonjour," Mata yelled a couple of times. A pair of boys typically worked the stables, but neither appeared to take the horse as they approached.

"Bessie, it appears to be just you and moi," she whispered to the animal in a soothing manner.

Jumping down from the saddle, she held onto the reins and led the horse through the large double doors of the stable. Strong odors filled the structure. She considered stepping back outside but resisted the urge and led Bessie to one of the vacant stalls.

"Pardon, mon amour but I have no idea of how to care for you now," she said, moving to the front of the animal and rubbing a hand along the horse's neck. "A beau cheval such as you should be pampered like moi."

Giving a hushed laugh, she exited the stall and started to leave, when a black silhouette appeared in the doorway. The fingers of his right hand caught her attention as they opened and curled, over and around a pistol.

"Monsieur, my horse needs tending to."

She hoped her business-like attitude would prompt a reaction, but the man stood, unmoving and staring at her. Mata took a step closer but stopped as the man mirrored her action. A change in the distance did little to improve the tension, but it did give her a better view.

"Joseph? Are you heading to the gun range? You'd best fly if you mean to get some shots off before dark." Her words came out calmly, but she was anything but relaxed inside. The man had stared daggers at her for days. She fought to control her breathing and tried to remember her theatrical training from her early days in Paris. "Perhaps I'll join you there. After all, I have to improve my skills if the Admiral is going to send me into Germany."

Although he did not raise the weapon, Joseph approached to within an arm's length. His words came out sharp and soaked with venom.

"My brother was an officer on one of our warships, the Minerva. There was an ambush. The bloody Germans had a line of U-Boats set up to pick off our ships. It wasn't just random chance that they picked that spot to spring their attack. You fucking whore, you gave them the shipping routes." His voice became raspy as his temper flared. "All those men, lost because you wanted money, wanted adventure, wanted to be an agent provocateur."

Mata glanced around, hoping that his ragged tone may draw the attention of someone nearby. Mentally, she pleaded for someone, anyone to step from the shadows, someone she had overlooked, but no one materialized.

"And worse, you play both sides. Can't even show any loyalty to one side or another. Just use men, get what you can and smile as you casually screw over innocent folks that happen to suffer because of your treachery."

Seeing the pistol starting to rise, Mata jumped to action. Remembering her training, she lashed out, grabbing his right wrist with her left hand, and smacking his throat hard with her right. Stunned, he staggered back, but her hand held his wrist firm. With a twist, she turned his gun hand around and then chopped at the wrist with her free hand. The sudden shock caused him to lose his grip, and the pistol fell to the hay-covered ground.

Jerking his arm free, he lashed out, smacking her hard across the face. Her vision flashed white as the pain hit her. Staggering back, she knew he had not gotten a good strike due to his position. Still, his blow hurt like hell.

"Damned whore!" he screamed and lunged forward.

Twisting, she kicked out with all her might, connecting her foot with his stomach. All the air in his lungs expelled in a sickening gasp and he staggered back, doubled over, clutching his gut.

"One way or another, you're not leaving here alive," he wheezed. Still hunched over, he stepped to the front wall and grabbed an axe that had been propped up beside the door.

Mata swallowed hard as he looked back at her, holding the weapon with both hands. His eyes seemed filled with the fury of the devil, and his grin implied the horror he meant for her. It was then that her hands began to shake, knowing that she could easily die here. She was alone and at the mercy of a madman.

Words that Mr. Jackson had drilled into her over and over during their hand-to-hand combat training flashed in the forefront of her mind. "In a fight, never lose focus on your surroundings. No matter how scared you are, always remember that there is a way out."

Glancing around, she spotted the pistol laying a few feet away where Joseph had dropped it. She looked up and saw him looking at it and then at her. She knew she could reach it first, and so did he. They leapt at the same time.

The cold steel felt alien in her hand, but she brought it to bear. He was six feet away, axe raised over his head, when she pulled the trigger. The weapon jerked in her hand, but she tightened her grip just in time to avoid losing it. The brilliant flash in the dimly lit barn blinded her momentarily. For a moment, she could only make out the indistinct movement of the man twisting around.

She blinked and saw him doubled over, his left arm squeezing his abdomen. The axe, still in his right hand, dragged across the ground as he stepped back. Her eyes were wide, and her heart felt like it would pound its way through her chest.

"You're gonna die, bitch!"

She smacked her dry mouth and tried to form words but could only get out a muted gasp.

Joseph lunged again, screaming, but the pistol fired two more times, illuminating the structure briefly with each shot. He grunted and fell back to the ground. Mata stood still, afraid to move but keeping the weapon raised and pointed at the dead man. Her hands shook wildly, and she dropped to one knee and tried to get her breathing under control.

"I think that's enough for one day." A man's voice echoed through the structure.

Three electric lightbulbs flashed to life, flooding the barn with illumination. Mata looked up at the front doorway to see the Admiral and Mr. Jackson entering. In stunned surprise, she jumped as Joseph rose to his feet. She immediately pointed the weapon and she stepped back, ready for anything.

"Miss Hari, that won't be necessary," the Admiral said as he strolled to the young man. "As always, my boy, a wonderful performance."

She swallowed hard and then studied Joseph. Three shots in the torso yet not a drop of blood. She twisted the pistol in her hand and inspected it.

"Blanks, my dear." Jackson approached and took the weapon from her. "It's full of blanks."

The Admiral spoke up, "This was a test, for lack

of a better word. You said you weren't a killer, so we needed to put that to the test." He looked at Joseph. "Three body shots, from what I could see. I'd call that a kill."

"Yes, sir. A kill indeed," Joseph added, smiling at her.

Her body, still charged with adrenalin, shook and her anger flared. "Test! I could have..." She paused and shook her head. "No, no. I could have killed..."

"Yes, my dear," The Admiral replied. "That was the point. And in theory, you did kill him."

Part Three: Journey into the Storm.

Mata lay back on the bed, smiling contently as the last shreds of her morning's first orgasm faded. Her hand moved to the young woman's head nestled between her thighs. Letting her fingers gently run through Bonnie's hair, she carefully rocked the girl's head to the right. Bonnie took the silent instruction and repositioned herself. The goddess had taught the girl what she loved most, and Bonnie had-not and would-not disappoint. Her tongue continued lapping with slow, deliberate strokes.

"Oui, mon cheri." Mata pushed the girl's head down as the pleasure rolled through her body in waves, breaking hard against her brain, like the sea against a rocky shoreline. Her normal composure, dominant and unyielding, began to fall apart as the threat of another orgasm grew quickly within her.

"Don't stop," Mata whispered over and over.

Her body shook and her limbs seemed useless. Looking at the ceiling, the morning's sun had flooded through the window, painting it a blinding orange. Like the room, her body felt as if it were on fire, warm and delicious flames consuming her.

"Oui, mon amour, oui!"

Mata could not help but cry out as the little death took her, slamming into her psyche like a freight train. Her body convulsed uncontrollably for what felt like an eternity. Then she went limp. Her closed eyes opened, but she did not care about the view. Her mind felt dulled and slow.

Bon Dieu, does this femme know how to please me.

Bonnie lifted herself from her place of worship,

moved on all fours, and positioned herself beside her Mistress. Mata leaned over and kissed Bonnie, tasting herself in the process.

"Merci, my pet."

Mata held Bonnie close for a while as their breathing slowed. She took in the young woman's smell and kissed her head and face, repeatedly. The small moan of satisfaction which escaped from between Bonnie's lips meant the world to Mata.

She glanced at the packed bags sitting beside the door and let out a groan. She had become accustomed to this place and the beautiful redhead who surrendered herself, body and soul, each night.

"When this is all over with, I want you to join me in Paris. A gem such as you could set the city on fire. And like any jewel in the rough, you just need to be perfectly cut and polished." Mata leaned in again, planting a long passionate kiss on her pet's lips. "And cutting and polishing are what I excel at."

A knock at the door made both heads turn. Without a second warning, the door opened, and Mr. Black stepped inside. He immediately turned to look elsewhere instead of at the women.

"Miss Cutler, we'll have words later. Ms Hari, the automobile is waiting. We have barely enough time to make it to the station."

Bonnie snatched up a sheet and covered herself, but Mata gave her a stern look. "My pet, he has been aware of your devotion to me for quite some time. You have no need to be shy or reserved around him from this point further."

Bonnie looked back and forth between the two and then stood, letting the sheet fall. Mr. Black impatiently turned and tried to keep from staring at the nude women. Mata laughed at his flustered appearance as she stood, snapped her fingers, and let her Irish pet dress her.

"What makes you think that I've known about... this?" he asked.

She grinned and nodded to the large mirror on the wall, "Do you think that a lady of refinement such as moi would not notice that you've placed a transparent mirror in her room?" She watched as he swallowed hard. "I'm sure you and your superiors have been enjoying our nightly performances." Mata reached out and let a finger run under Bonnie's chin. "And I'm sure you've been listening in on the conversations between Bonny and myself, but she said nothing about this mirror, did she? Well, Monsieur Black, this room isn't the only place we've conversed. My pet told me all about your mirrors, listening devices, and concerns about my loyalty."

He cleared his throat and looked uncomfortable. "It was all part of the... what I mean to say is..."

"Bonnie, be a dear and fetch me a pasty, preferably one with blueberries inside. I'll finish here and snack on the ride to the station. But do put on one of my robes. No point in giving the entire kitchen staff a view of your lovelies." Mata said and watched the woman nod and scurry off.

With Bonny gone, Black sighed and shook his head. "I must confess, we're in awe of what you've done with her."

Mata laughed, "In or out of the bed?"

"She wasn't asked to come here. She did that on her own, but once it started, we watched and observed the process. All I can say is, remarkable." Mr. Black said. "Is this enslavement process, the hypnosis, meant to be permanent?"

"Only if she wishes it to be," Mata said as she

straightened her silk stockings and slipped on her shoes. "You see, some have the desire, the mental fortitude to lead. Others, such as our dear Bonnie, find contentment and joy in serving others. I suspect that she will come to me in Paris after this is over and turn her back on King and Country in order to serve her goddess. You see, deep down inside, it's what she truly wants to do."

"And the men you seduce? They want to submit?" Black inquired.

"I can usually size a man up after speaking with him for a short while. If he is weak, he'll be mine. If not, I give him a night of pleasure he'll never forget."

Black looked surprised. "But if he isn't going to give you what you want, then why bother?"

"Because, my dear Monsieur Black, men naturally brag about sex. A strong man may not yield his secrets to me, but if he is in a position of power, he may tell his weak friends about me. They'll seek me out. And from them, I'll gather my secrets to sell."

"And what of me? Your opinion?"

"Unlike what the Admiral thinks, it wasn't fear that kept you in line during our trip." Mata walked to him, took his left hand and pulled It to her. A well painted nail tapped the shiny gold band on his ring finger. "Your marriage is still young and full of love. It is untarnished by time and the boring routines of day-to-day life." She briefly thought about her own marriage and added, "Believe me when I say I hope it remains as it is now."

Several minutes later, Mata and Mr. Black supervised the loading of her luggage into the back of the rumbling auto. The smell of its exhaust did not sit well with her, nor did the mission to come. Bonnie stepped from the front door and Mata held her arms open, hugging her tightly as soon as her pet stepped close enough. Tears already marked both women's cheeks.

"Your pastry." Bonnie handed a cloth-covered sweet to Mata and then wiped her eyes. "I got exactly what you wanted."

Mata kissed her and said, "I'll be back in Paris in a few weeks. I'll expect you to come when I message you." They kissed again and she whispered, "You belong to me, mon amour. I will miss you greatly."

Half an hour later, Mata and Mr. Black left the car behind, boarding the same train she had arrived on to begin the journey to Penzance. The passenger car held only herself, Black, and a pair of soldiers. She wondered if they were bodyguards, here to protect her from the famers of the countryside.

"What happens if I fail?" She asked.

Mr. Black, whose attention had been focused on the blurry images of the passing countryside, sat up. "Excuse me?"

Letting out a frustrated breath, she repeated the question. "What happens if I fail to kill him? Do you have… what is it called, a backup plan?"

He swallowed and looked sheepish, "I'm not sure."

"Are you saying you don't know, or that there is no other way?"

"I'm say that you are our only way to get close. If you fail, we have no other asset in place to take a crack at killing him."

She looked down at her fidgeting hands, "So I can't afford to fail."

"Don't think of it in that regard. You'll fill your

head with doubt and worry. That kind of thing can rattle the best of agents when the moment arrives. You've been well-trained and you are ready. Just keep telling yourself that you can do it." He reached out and placed his hands over hers. When she looked up, he smiled and gave a reassuring nod. "You're Mata Hari, after all, and the General is just a man. What chance does he have against you?"

She forced a smile and spoke with feigned confidence. "True. He'll never know what hit him."

The train ride ended, and another fast civilian cruiser took to the seas. The ship sailed east through the Channel, staying clear of the French coastline.

For days, the plan had been drilled into her head. A fast boat would take her to the French port of Dunkirk. From there, it would be a quick jaunt into Paris so that she could make an appearance and announce plans to travel abroad. She would then travel by secured transport to Brussels where she would be able to catch a train into Germany.

But that plan was not to be.

Mata stood on the deck, leaning slightly over the railing to see the bow slicing through the blue waters. Her hair danced in the wind, much to her delight. Glancing back over her shoulder, she noticed several of the crew watching and enjoying her presence. Mister Black emerged from the ship's radio shack and strolled towards her, holding a small paper.

Black read over the telegraphed message as he approached and sighed. "The situation has changed."

"What sort of change?" she asked.

"Our original sources predicted that General Kripker wouldn't be heading back to the front for another month. Seems he's apparently resting up from a severe wound to his leg. But we've gotten word that the old war horse is boarding a train in two days and heading back to the German lines near Albert for a major push against Amiems. If the Germans capture the city, it'll erase many of the advances we've made over the past year and a half."

Mata considered this, "How can I get to him now?"

"We'll make port at Le Crotoy, from there we'll catch a train and head south to the British airfields outside of Abbeville." He cleared his throat and looked apprehensively at her. "From there, the only way is by air."

"Air? As in getting into one of those flying kites?" She exclaimed. "They're nothing but sticks and canvas."

"We'll have a pilot and a secure aircraft ready and waiting. He'll fly you to Liege where you can meet Kripker's train." She glared at him as he continued. "We've already spread word in Paris that you've returned to The Hague for family business and that you're planning a trip south afterwards. Your German handlers in Paris have already passed it on, so your appearance in Liege will not be surprising."

"If I say no to this?" Mata said, crossing her arms and narrowing her eyes.

He lit a cigarette and looked at her in a way which unnerved Mata to no end. "You know what my government is prepared to do in order to assure your cooperation. But if it'll sweeten the deal, when this is over and you are safely back in your Paris apartment, I'll personally bring Bonnie to you. What you've done to her worked incredibly well. We had to threaten her with restraints to keep her from trying to come with us. She's become very loyal to you very quickly."

She reached over and snatched the cigarette from his fingers and took a long draw on it. Letting the smoke billow out from her full lips, she nodded and thought about the nights with her pet.

"A good bargain, I suppose. I claim her life as my own in exchange for taking his. There is a strange form of karma at play in all of this. I lose a life that has importance to me but gain a new one in its place."

A few hours later, storm clouds billowed on the southern horizon, covering the French countryside as the ship drifted into port. Mata stood on the deck, watching the flashes of lightning as they illuminated the wafting columns of vapor in various shades of oranges and reds.

"It'll hit us soon." Mr. Black approached from behind. He set down their luggage and leaned against the railing with her.

"We still have a little time before the ship is moored," she said, nodding to the bags.

"I'm not taking chances. As soon as the gangplank is in place, we're moving. We've got to get you south as quickly as we can."

They watched in silence as the ship moved into place, assisted by a slow-moving tug. Once snug and secured, the walkway was moved up. Before it could even be locked in place, the pair were running down it, bags in hand.

"Do you know where we're going?" she asked, trying to keep up with him on the crowded pier.

The crowds came from nowhere and all seemed destined for the ship they had just left. Mata turned and watched for a moment. The bulk of the people were elderly folks, women, and children; all looked like they had been living on the streets for years. Most had dirty clothing and unkempt hair. What pained her the most were the number wearing bloody bandages.

Black grabbed her arm. "They're mostly refugees from Belgium or the German-occupied territories. They have nowhere left to go except to find sanctuary on the other side of the Channel."

She gave in to his tugs and followed, never letting her eyes connect with the rag-tag group that ran and fought for passage away from this Hell-enshrined land. Gunfire erupted from behind her and she heard screams.

"Keep moving. The faster we can get to the train station, the better off we'll be. Assuming the trains are able to move south."

"Moving? You don't know if they're moving?" she yelled.

"This isn't like your peaceful little palace in Paris. The front lines are constantly shifting, one way or another. The people around here have learned to move fast and on a moment's notice. Trains, however, can only move where their tracks allow. So, if a section of the line falls into German hands, the trains don't move."

Mata's heart beat harder. It was not the physical exertion. She could easily keep up with Black's fast pace. Instead, something about the crowd terrified her. The faces, unhealthy and panicked, all desperate for escape, rattled her understanding of the war. She had seen some signs of panic and fear in Paris early in the war, when the Germans seemed unstoppable and were nearly at the city's metaphorical gates. But that was nothing compared to this, a wave of terrified people who had no homes, no belongings, and from the expressions some wore, no hope in the future.

Reaching the train station, half an hour later, Mata found that it was in no better shape than the docks. Hundreds of people shouted, waving cash and treasures in the air in hopes that they could secure a seat on the west-bound trains.

"You there!" Black shouted to an overwhelmed porter. "I'm a member of His Majesty's government, and it is imperative that the lady and I obtain passage south to Abbeville."

The middle-aged porter shrugged his shoulders, "Everyone here is important, or so they claim. You'll have to take your chances at the ticket booths, like everyone else."

"You don't understand. This is vital!" Black shouted again over the roar of the surrounding crowd.

The porter glanced around and began to wave Black away when he spotted Mata. His eyes lit up and a strange smile appeared on his weathered face.

"Mata Hari? Is that really you?" She nodded and he pushed a few folks aside to get closer to her. "I saw you years ago, dancing at *l'Olympia*. I have several of your photographs."

Mata's ego swelled as it always did when hearing accolades from admirers of her dancing. Seeing his excited expression, she let her charms loose on the man. Smiling, she gave him a nod, gesturing the man closer.

"My friend is sincere when he says we must

obtain passage south. Please tell me that you can help me." Closer to him now, she snaked an arm around his waist and pulled him close enough to whisper directly into his ear. "If you can make this happen, you'll always have a special seat to every performance I give when you're in Paris."

His eyes widened as did the smile on his face. "Right this way, Madame. Let me see what I can do."

He stepped to another porter and waved them to follow. He led the pair into the railyard and toward what at first appeared to be a rusted-out, abandoned locomotive, attached to a pair of rickety passenger cars. From the faded paint and weathered wood, the cars looked to be decades old.

"This one is up next to depart. We're having to press these older engines into service. The Army has priority over all the newer ones."

Mata and Black were the first passengers on board the disheveled passenger car. A pungent smell almost gagged her, but she smiled to her savior in appreciation.

The porter waved a hand, "Take any seat you wish. The other passengers will be coming along soon, and I expect it'll be rather crowded, but it'll get you to your destination."

"Why are so many people here?" She asked Black. "Do they know the Germans are going to make a big push?"

Black led her to the back of the car and waited until she sat before taking his seat.

"A big push? Madame, they are always pushing and we in turn are always pushing back. But given the chaos, I'd imagine that someone has leaked German intentions and the news is spreading, no doubt blown completely out of proportion. But this sort of thing isn't uncommon."

The train ride should have only taken an hour, but Black explained that the engineer kept the speed low, to watch for breaks in the line from stray artillery shells or sabotage. The thunderstorm did not help either. The train cars rocked harder as the harsh winds buffeted them and the heavens seemed to dump oceans in the form of large, heavy rain drops that came down from the skies, almost sideways. Four hours later, they slowed to a stop, a few miles outside of Abbeville.

Mata watched the rain for a while until the downpour subsided. "Maybe now we'll resume our journey."

Groans erupted from the crowds at the front of the car. Voices spoke, some loudly, complaining about the delay. A pair of voices relayed the news to everyone. A tree had fallen across the tracks. Men were working to clear it, but it would take time.

Mr. Black grabbed her hand. "Time to go. The airfield is a mile or so from here. It'll be quicker on foot than waiting until we start up again."

Mata did not argue, although her stomach churned at the idea of flying. Black grabbed up her bag and stepped from the car. She looked out at the open countryside, pockmarked with burnt-out craters from the never-ending shelling that Eastern France had endured. The walk was not as hard as she first thought it would be, even carrying one of her bags. Despite the thick mud and pooling rainwater, once away from the tracks, the land flattened. They were able to quicken their pace over the grassy fields. A curious thought occurred to Mata.

"How could an airfield have survived out here for so long, with all the shelling?"

Black laughed, "This field was established a month ago. Once this land had been taken back and the trenches and craters filled in, it made an amenable place for aircraft to land and take-off. And it's close enough to the front lines to make for short flights."

The smell of death and decay wafted on the wind, making Mata turn her head sharply. Black looked around as well.

She scanned the broken landscape. "Is that a man's body producing the odor?"

Black replied, "It doesn't matter. We have to keep moving."

"Is it a man? A body?"

Black stopped and looked at her. "In battles as vast as these, most of the fallen are collected. But it only makes sense that a few may be overlooked. Or...."

"Or what?" she asked.

"If a mortar shell explodes next to a soldier, there may not be enough pieces big enough to pick up. The whole area is no doubt covered in parts."

She nodded and tried to hold her breath.

"Let's get moving then. It should be a short walk from here." Black said.

As they reached the crest of a small ridgeline, the airfield came into view, much to Mata's relief. A gust of wind surrounded the pair in the stench of death again. Suddenly, the thought of flying away from this place did not scare her in the least.

Mata stood watching the men of the airfield going about their daily routines. A small army of workers engaged in maintenance on the two rows of biplanes. A trio of men sat outside a nearby bar, which Black had disappeared into. Given their conversations, they were pilots. Knights of the sky, as the papers like to call them.

The damp air made her shiver slightly, but as the clouds moved further away, the warmth of the sun returned. She loved the image of the dark storm front, now moving off behind her, while the few remaining puffs of white followed. The edges of these glowed from the bright sun. It looked like the flight path, or at least what she knew of it, would steer clear of the bad weather.

Exhausted from the walk, she let her mind wander briefly until the sounds of footfalls, splashing through the mud and standing water, brought her gaze around to Black.

"Miss Hari, I'd like you to meet Lieutenant Scarborough," Black said as he and a young dark-haired man approached. "He'll be flying you to a spot just outside of Liege."

"Mr. Black tells me that time is of the essence." He spoke with a British accent. Glancing at a pocket watch, he shrugged. "We have a few of hours of light left. The Secret Service boys will have a special landing area lit up for us. If you'll give me the lady's bags, I'll load them aboard and get Rosalita ready to go."

"You'll get who ready?" Mata asked.

"My plane, ma'am."

Black handed Mata's bag to the pilot, who quickly walked to a nearby fighter plane. He then turned to Mata and extended a hand. She took it and then pulled Black close and hugged him tightly. She knew the hug meant little to him, but in that moment, he was the only man that could spare her the hell that was to come. Realizing that she had clung to him a little too long, she stepped back. Seeing his expression, she realized he could see the fear on hers.

"Ms Hari, trust me when I tell you that Scarborough is one of our best pilots. He'll get you there. Besides, most of the squadron will be escorting you across no-man's land." He looked back at the plane momentarily as its engine cranked up. "Once on the ground, a woman named Gertrude will ferry you to Liege. She is already making arrangements with our people there to connect you, in some form or fashion, to General Kripker."

Mata looked at the plane and felt an icy chill of panic fire its way through her.

"You'll be fine. Just breath, relax, and remember that you're in good hands." A smile appeared on Black's face. "Besides, you wouldn't want Scarborough to come back and talk about the Great Mata Hari being afraid of flying, would you?"

She shook her head and swallowed hard, "No. Mr. Black, for what it's worth, it's been a pleasure. If you'll allow…" She stepped closer and kissed him on the cheek. "Tell your wife that she is one lucky woman."

It felt like her stomach fell as the Bristol F.2 fighter plane pulled away from the ground and leapt skyward. Eight other planes, following behind, left with them. Their mission was twofold, from what the lieutenant explained. They would escort her through the heavens until their aircraft reached the German lines, and then the others would leave them and cover a bombing mission along the front.

Sitting in the rear seat, she faced the back of the plane. Instead of seeing where they were going, her view was of where they had been. Still, watching the accompanying aircraft was a bit of a joy. As a woman who had never left the Earth, her view of planes had been looking up at their bottoms. Now she could study the way they seemed to dance, bouncing and such, while staying in a tight formation. Only the damned gun obstructed her view. She had been briefed, quickly before leaving, on how to use the rear facing Lewis machine gun. Not that she or her pilot expected that to be necessary.

Even an hour into the flight, the feeling in her gut had not returned to normal. With goggles in place, Mata had an incredible view of the surrounding countryside as they passed overhead. But as the plane approached the frontline, the ground below became darker, scorched and broken. For miles in every direction, fresh bomb craters pockmarked the land. She thought about the long-lasting wounds mankind had inflicted on Mother Earth.

Soldiers, like ants, scurried to and fro, like ants, while puffs of black smoke appeared and vanished. She could not hear the distant explosions or gunfire. The roar of the winds almost deafened her, but when the pilot began shouting, his words came across very clear.

"Enemy fighters straight ahead!"

Her stomach bounced as the plane lurched back and forth. She looked around and watched as the other British fighters began pitching up or down, preparing and positioning themselves to plunge into the coming dogfight.

Scarborough turned partly around and yelled back. "The machine gun back there. Sorry, Miss, but I'll have to press you into action. If we pick up a Jerry on our tail, you may need to fire it. Grab the bolt— that thing sticking out on the side and pull it back. Then aim and pull the trigger."

The noise of a thousand screams echoed around her as the plane increased speed. Small streaks of light shot past the plane. Turning slightly, she spotted the Germans planes barreling in, their guns ablaze. German triplanes swarmed into the British formation. Gunfire flew in every direction. Mata sat, frozen as she watched the sky suddenly became alive with streaking lights, each one with the potential to kill instantly.

The plane jerked violently to the right and the nose pulled up, causing her sink back into the seat. The plane pushed up and then fell back, and for a moment, Mata experienced the world upside down. As they began to dive, she struggled to look around, but saw nothing at first. The force of the maneuver made moving difficult as the gravity seemed to double, pushing down on her chest and making breathing difficult. This was a sensation she had never experienced before, and it made breathing hard. Thudding noises from bullets impacting the wing told her what was happening. Getting on her knees in the seat, she turned and saw a green plane, brandishing black and white iron crosses on its wings, occasionally coming into view as both aircraft danced in their chase.

I'm going to die, she thought, but another bullet strike, this one near her seat, erased her fear and replaced it with anger. *I will not die like a coward without a fight.*

She jerked the bolt on the machine gun back as she had been taught, released it, and took aim. The mounted gun sprayed out three shots when her finger pulled back on the trigger. Looking down the sights to aim seemed all but pointless, given the way she was being tossed about. But every third round fired was a tracer. Instead of lead, the round fired a sliver of burning phosphorous which glowed and left a streaking trail. The glowing round made it easy enough for her to see as it shot over the German plane.

She remembered Jackson's training about anticipating her movements and those of her target. Pulling the trigger, she moved the weapon around, spraying a stream of lead back. The German bounced around, but Mata's aim proved to be reasonably true. The Fokker tri-plane zig-zagged through her shots until it jerked hard right, rolled over with fire spouting from the engine, and dropped downward.

Another German zoomed down from above, its machine guns blazing. Scarborough jerked the plane to the left and banked, giving her a change to turn the gun downward and squeeze off a few shots before it was too far away. Looking around, she saw only four of the Brits still flying, two of which were chasing the lone German, which now belched a thick torrent of smoke as it dropped toward the broken earth below. The sky was marred with wafting strands of black smoke, curving and dancing about, but eventually leading downward.

"I think we're good," Scarborough shouted back to her.

The afternoon sun descended in the west, illuminating the edges of the storm clouds they had left behind them. As frightened as she was about flying, Mata had to admit to herself that the view was perhaps the most beautiful thing she had ever seen. Relaxing back into her seat, she looked up and saw the first stars of the evening as they came into view.

"About another five minutes or so," Scarborough shouted back. He pointed to an area ahead but a little to the right. "There! I can see the landing spot."

Mata looked in the direction he pointed and in the far distance, she could make out a short string of lights on a patch of farmland. She heard the plane's engine roar lessen as they slowed and began dropping altitude.

As they lowered, the sky seemed darker. The tree lines, flanking the field, cast long, dark shadows across the land, which would make the landing tricky. When the wheels touched down, the aircraft shuddered violently, and Mata yelped in fear that the plane may break apart. The engine shut off as soon as the wheels hit the ground. The craft rolled a short way before coming to a stop.

The sudden silence unnerved Mata. After a day of yelling, screaming, roaring engines and gunfire, the quiet surrounded her, encasing her in a private universe of her own. At least for a few moments, anyway.

"Douse the lanterns, you little fools," A man's voice yelled out.

Looking from her seat as the plane, a group of four boys ran about, extinguishing the small flames in the lanterns that lined the makeshift landing strip. An elderly man and woman approached the plane. Scarborough tossed her bags to the ground and then climbed out. Mata followed behind, thanking the heavens to be on firm ground again.

"This way. We have precious little time." The woman grabbed Mata's arm and tugged her hard. "We have a wagon waiting. Geordi, grab the lady's bags." she shouted to one of the boys.

"Wagon?" she looked back to the men. They, along with the boys, began pushing the plane toward the trees. "Lieutenant Scarborough."

The pilot turned and waved. "We have no time. Godspeed to you."

"But what about you?" she asked.

"I'll refuel and take off at dawn, assuming the krauts didn't see us land," he said, and waved goodbye.

Somewhat disappointed, Mata turned and let the old woman lead her through the trees. The line was not thick, and she could easily see the horse-drawn wagon, partially loaded with a mound of hay. The boy ran ahead and tossed her bags in the back of it and then climbed on board. Burrowing into the loose straw, the bags were stuffed into the mound and covered up.

"We'll take you to the outskirts of town and then we walk to the hotel from there," the woman said.

Mata nodded as she climbed onto the bench seat. She looked over at the woman, who stared back, unamused. "Is there a room waiting on me?"

"Yes. I'll escort you to the hotel. A friend of the Brits will write something up for the local paper about your arrival in town. That should spread news of your presence in town all over the place by the time the German train arrives."

One Life for Another

"What time will that be?" Mata asked.

"General Kripker's train should arrive late tomorrow night. That should give you time to contact the German officers in town and ask for an audience with him."

"And if I can't get to him?

Gertrude looked back at her. "I don't know. All I do know is to get you to the hotel so you can meet with the General."

The woman smacked the reins down on the horse's hindquarters. With a jerk, the wagon began to move. An unusual odor made Mata's nose twitch. It only took a moment for her to realize the odor came from the old woman.

The stars were on full display thirty minute later when they arrived in Liege. The city, for the most part was unlit and eerily quiet. Aside from their wagon, the place appeared deserted. Only a handful of lights in the many buildings were illuminated, but the streetlights were blazing.

"Where is everyone?" Mata asked.

Gertrude explained. "There is a curfew in place to keep people off the streets." She pointed to the streetlights. "They keep those on all night. It allows the occupying German soldiers to keep a better watch for spies and saboteurs. The French may love peace, but when our freedom is taken, we fight back."

"What happens if they catch us?" Mata said in a hushed tone.

Gertrude snorted. "I have you. If they ask, your train was stopped, and you needed a ride to reach the city in time to meet the General."

Mata cocked an eyebrow in disbelief. "And that'll do it?"

"I cook meals for the many of the guards and several officers. They pay me almost nothing, but it keeps me in good graces with them. I'd mentioned your arrival earlier, so they should swallow my lies as quickly as they do my bread." Gertrude pointed at one of the buildings in the distance. "There it is."

"Are they catching many spies?" Mata's voice was barely a whisper.

"The Kaiser feels that we caused too many delays in their plans to take Paris. As if invading our land wasn't cause for us to fight back. No matter, I suppose. They've been killing anyone after dark, except yours truly. I'm often called in by the officers at all hours, to cater get-togethers. But other townsfolk, they are not so lucky. It's our so-called punishment for their failures." Gertrude said.

She pulled the wagon into a dark alley between a pair of warehouses. Even the moonlight dared not follow them in there, or so it seemed to Mata.

"From here, we need to be more cautious." Gertrude whispered.

The ladies abandoned the wagon and began walking. Moving fast, they darted from alley to alley, carefully watching for German patrols and guards. The quiet of the city unnerved her. Paris was a city where parties and celebrations lasted all night, every night. This city felt dead.

It was midnight when they reached the hotel. The desk clerk eyed her suspiciously until a glimmer of recognition appeared.

"Madam Hari? It is an honor to have you here," he said as he pushed a key across the counter. "There's been whispers of your planned visit to our beloved city. Our finest room is complimentary for someone as renowned as yourself. Will you be staying long?" His eyes darted back and forth between her and the old woman.

"Only a couple of days." She smiled and nodded to the old woman. "Gertrude was kind enough to give me a ride into town after the train I was aboard was stopped due to sabotage," Mata said.

Snapping his fingers, he waved a bellboy over to assist Mata to the room. The young man looked about eleven or twelve and escorted them to the elevator. A short ride and they emerged on the third floor. He said nothing, just opened the door and smiled at the ladies.

"Are you not the sweetest young man," Mata said and leaned over, kissing him on the cheek and pressing a coin into his hand.

Gertrude followed her into the plush room. The old woman looked around, mouth agape and eyes wide.

"I've never seen the likes. It's like a palace in here. Is this what you're always used too?" She asked and Mata laughed.

"Now a days, yes. In the past, though, my furnishings were quite different. I grew up in poverty and despair."

Both women looked toward the bathroom. Stepping to the doorway, Mata turned on the light and squealed.

"They have hot water. A relaxing bath is exactly what I need."

Mata turned and looked at Gertrude. The woman wore a dark expression.

From a pocket in her faded dress, Gertrude pulled long metal tube, a cigar holder. "Listen. They asked me to help with, well, with making sure you didn't fall prey to the Germans. So, I brought you this. The tobacco has been treated with a concoction that when smoked and inhaled will cause death, a quick and painless death. The poison is hard to trace so it'll look like natural causes. If you think they are going to imprison you or worse, smoke it." She handed it to Mata. "I don't know about you, but there are some things worse than death. And if you don't think you can get to the General, maybe you can pass this along and take care of him that way."

"Thank you and good luck to you," Mata said.

With Gertrude gone, Mata suddenly felt all alone. The crushing weight of her mission came to her and seemed to keep the breath from her lungs. She fell on the bed and let the events of the day replay in her head, and then promptly fell asleep.

Mata slept till noon the following day, only awakening when the maid knocked on her door. Slowly, she rose.

"Oui. Enter," Mata called as she stumbled across the room, and disappeared into the bathroom.

Taking a quick bath and dressing, she thought about the day ahead. She left the spacious bathroom, tugging at her dress just as the maid finished making the bed.

"Where is the German Command's headquarters?" Mata asked. The middle-aged woman recoiled a bit at the brazen question.

"Two blocks, north, madam."

Mata smiled as she walked to the small writing desk and scribbled a note. Turning, she grabbed her purse and waved the maid to her. Extracting a couple of francs, she pressed them and the note into the woman's hand.

"Take this to the Germans. Tell them that Mata Hari sent you." She looked into the woman's eyes and saw fear.

"No. I can't. They might throw me in jail." The maid began to visibly shake.

How bad things must be to incite such fear in this one. Mata thought.

Grabbing two more bills from her purse, Mata asked again. The maid looked at the money and finally agreed.

"I am told you wish an audience with General Kripker," the German officer said.

"Oui."

Mata glanced around the military office. The Germans had taken a mansion formerly belonging to one of the city's elite and turned it into their headquarters for this section of the small country.

The snooty officer removed his monocle and let his gaze move back and forth between her written request to see the General and her snug-fitting black dress. This time, his smile made her feel unclean.

"As I told your messenger earlier, German officers, especially ones as important as Otto Kripker, don't just meet with civilians, especially entertainers."

Mata narrowed her eyes as she spoke. "The General and I are old acquaintances."

"Frauline Hari. I can pass on your request, but unless I know the purpose, I can't make any assurances. The General is a busy man. Everyone thinks they should monopolize his time with their petty concerns."

This time it was Mata who gave a smile that unnerved him. "I don't know if my dear Otto would like to have my purpose disclosed. He and I are old friends. I'm sure you understand."

He gave a slight laugh that hinted at his discomfort. "I'll pass your request to his attaché. If you'd be so good as to return to your hotel. We'll collect you, should he wish to see you."

With that done, all she could do was return to the hotel and wait. The day passed without a word, but as the sun fell below the horizon, Mata heard a lone automobile pull up outside the hotel. Sitting on the small balcony, she peered down on the unstylish black sedan. A German officer stepped from the back, glancing up at the hotel and seeing her looking back at him.

She felt sick to her stomach at the sight of his nonchalant expression. Minutes later, a hard knock at the hotel room door startled her, even though it was expected. Her fears and nerves had gotten the better of her while she had waited.

"Yes?" She stepped back from the door as a pair of men entered the room, glancing around suspiciously.

A partially balding man stepped forward. "Frauline Hari, I am Major Schmidt. General Kripker would like for you to join him on his private train car. He's requested that you bring your bags, since he plans on having you join him for the journey to Albert."

"I wasn't expecting to be traveling." She could

see from their expressions that her fears were apparent. "I planned on performing in the coming days."

"There is no need to be alarmed, frauline. The General has a luxurious passenger car and you'll be his guest. And you need not fear about the fighting. You'll be nowhere near the battle zones. As for your shows, I'm certain the theatre owners will understand and reschedule for a later date."

Nodding, she quickly repacked her bag and followed the men to the awaiting car. Mata prayed they did not search her bag. Hidden within a secret pouch was a small, silenced handgun. She might be able to convince them it was merely for self-defense, but it was the only weapon she had. The poisoned cigar lay within there as well. Gertrude's words about using it came to mind. A deep-seated fear of imprisonment gnawed at her and she toyed with the idea of keeping the small tube in a pocket instead of the bag, just in case.

They made good time driving across town. Guards were everywhere when they reached the train station and continued past the terminal buildings. The car wove through the train yard, coming to a stop beside one of the passenger cars attached to an enormous, armored military locomotive.

"Follow me, Fraulein," Major Schmidt said.

She climbed out and followed the German officer as another followed behind her, carrying her bag. They stepped up the three steps at one end of the dark green train car, knocked, and then entered.

"General, as you requested, Miss Hari."

Mata stepped into the car and could not help but smile.

He sat in front of a small writing desk mounted to the car's right-side wall.

"General, so wonderful to see you." She watched the General smile as he approached.

A brute of a figure, his chest and arms were as muscular as a college athlete. His hair, grayer now than she remembered, was cut short. And as always, his uniform was clean and appeared as new as the day it was made.

"Mata, my dearest, I'm so glad you came to me," he said, limping towards her on his wounded leg. Smiling, he took her into his arms. As he hugged her, he said in a lower tone, "Gentlemen, if you'll give me and the lady some privacy."

Mata stepped away from his embrace and glanced back at the men as they withdrew from the car. Her bag was placed on the floor, near the door. Once alone, she stepped back into his arms.

"Otto, it is so good to see you." She wrapped her arms around him and pushed her lips to his.

"Oh, excuse me." The timid voice came from behind the General.

Mata tilted her head to get a view of who spoke. The voice had been so high, she was not sure if it was a man or a woman. Then the stories of the General's slave girls came to mind, but she was shocked to see a young man, maybe in his mid-teens standing there, with a stack of folders in his arms.

"Victor, you may retire for the rest of the evening. Wake me at seven and have breakfast for two prepared. And as I'd mentioned, the lady will be joining us for the next few weeks, so make any arrangements necessary."

"Yes, sir," the young man said as he stepped by them and proceeded out the door.

"A steward?"

The General laughed, "You know the German Army refuses to allow their ranking officers a chance to go in the field without sending along someone to make sure we know how to wipe our own asses."

Mata felt puzzled. "I'd assumed you'd have…"

"Have what?" he asked, pulling her close again.

"I'd heard rumors that you'd collected a harem of girls to do your bidding."

He laughed, "A harem? Nonsense." He kissed her lightly and added, "You know of my womanizing. We've enjoyed many nights together, and I'll admit there have been a few others from time to time, but a harem? Really, Mata. Do you think the Kaiser allows his officers to have those kinds of luxuries?"

Mata slowly shook her head. "I would imagine not." She paused then added, "Others?"

"Yes, but you knew that. Distractions really, since none of them could live up to the high standards you set."

He kissed her again, but this time, Mata let herself be taken. Old feelings stirred within her and her heart raced. Thoughts of the mission danced near the forefront of her mind, but she pushed them down. There would be time for that later. Now, she only wanted to enjoy what time she had left with him.

She carefully began undressing him, taking her time, peeling off the jacket then his shirt. Reaching around him from behind, her fingers moved up his torso, parting the salt and pepper hair on his chest. Her head tilted forward, letting her lips touch and caress the back of his neck and shoulders with scores of small kisses.

Stepping around and in front of him, Mata did not stop her kissing, although as his scent filled her nostrils, she did let her teeth lightly graze him. Their lips met. The kiss felt to her like it lasted for an eternity. He grabbed her forcibly, pulling her closer. She let her arms drop to her sides as he held her firmly in place.

As their lips parted, Mata whispered, "I surrender, mon general."

In a hushed tone, he responded. "Mata, how I've missed the taste of your lips."

"Just the taste?"

He cocked an eyebrow as his lips moved to match the smirk she wore. "Show me what I've really missed."

Going to her knees, she removed his boots, placing them carefully to the side, then unfastened his belt and pants. Quickly, she undressed him and without hesitation, took him into her mouth. It took little effort on her part to bring his manhood fully to life. As she looked, he rewarded her with a low moan, showing his appreciation of her skill.

Without warning, he pulled himself back and grabbed her. "No. Not yet."

He maneuvered her to the bed, but she spun him around and slowly pushed him into the mass of pillows and blankets. "Lie down, mon amour."

As he watched, Mata stepped back. Lifting her arms, she began to move, dancing to a tune she replayed in her head. Slowly, her body turned and twisted, hypnotically drawing his eyes to her. Skillfully, her clothing dropped to the floor, one piece at a time. Moving to him, their lips met again. She ignited flames within him as her hand massaged him back to life. She kissed his lips, then kissed down his chest and stomach until she found a stopping point. He moaned as she worked him again, letting her lips worship the man.

When she had him properly prepared, Mata moved and rolled over onto her back, beside him. He preferred certain things, a favorite of which was looking down into her eyes as he took her.

The General kissed her briefly as he rose and positioned himself. With a moan, he pushed into her. Mata's passion grew as the man worked himself in her. All the cares of the world left her as he pushed her over the brink, time and time again. Hours seemed like minutes to the lovers, but exhaustion finally slowed their movements and rest was needed.

They lay side by side, his arm around her, as her fingers lightly caressed his chest.

"You are the only man who can so easily satisfy me." Mata said. He gave a curt laugh and she continued. "Otto, I don't know what to do."

He looked at her. "I can tell something is bothering you. Tell me what is on you mind."

"After the war. What do you want to do after the war?"

His fingers stopped their movements and a deep sigh left him. "It is hard to say. Not that I don't know, but for me, it is hard to admit."

She looked up into his eyes. "Please."

"Mata, I've been a soldier all my life. I've fought and killed for my country, my King, my Kaiser. And for what? This war should have lasted months, and it's been years. Millions of our finest men have died, cut down in the prime of life." He paused and cleared his throat. "After victory or defeat, I plan on retiring. I can't do this anymore. Not for a man like Wilhelm. He's a hot-headed fool. We'd never have gotten into this nightmare if not for him."

"Otto, what happens to the army after the war?"

"If we win, I retire, and another man takes my place. I would think that the soldiers will be stationed throughout the conquered lands until an amiable set of peace terms are set into place."

Mata nodded and asked, "And if you lose?"

"If we lose? There will be no army to worry about."

Mata nodded and laid her head back on his chest.

"My dearest, what is this all about?"

"I was picked up by the British Secret Service and given an option, be jailed and executed as a spy or...," she paused and considered if telling him was the right thing. The look in his eyes, such concern for her, made the decision an easy one. "Or kill you."

He remained still except for the fingers that played with her. "That wasn't fair of them to make you choose. And since you are here, I assume you made your choice?"

"Otto, they are frightened of you. They've gotten word from sources in Berlin that you plan on disbanding your army." Mata said. She quickly explained everything the British knew about him and his plans for after the war ended.

"Mata, that is madness. I would never do such a thing. If anything, I'm putting pressure on the Kaiser to make peace as soon as possible, before we are truly defeated. Only a fool can't see where this is all heading, and our Kaiser is just such a fool."

"I have to let England know about this. Someone is feeding them false information." Mata said and sat up.

"It'll be difficult, but I can arrange something. A private messenger perhaps." Kripker ran a hand along her back and added, "Thank you. Thank you for being honest about your purpose here."

One Life for Another

She looked at him and smiled. "I love you, Otto. I always have."

The door swung open and Major Schmidt and another officer entered, holding pistols.

'What is the meaning of this?" Kripker demanded, sitting up beside Mata.

Closing the door behind them, Schmidt glared at her and Kripker. "The Kaiser has become aware of this cowardly streak that has developed in your thinking. He's grown tired of your pushes for peace, your constant calls for a negotiation. He demands victory, and yet his officers continue to fail him. You continue to fail him."

"We fail him because he asks for too much and interferes in all the details of the planning," Kripker said. "If the bastard would have kept his nose out of the military's work, France would have fallen in the first year. But look what his meddling has achieved."

"Don't insult our Kaiser. He is a great man and you've failed him," Schmidt said.

Mata smirked, "Of course, the Kaiser. He's the one who let the British think Otto was some major threat, so they'd find a way to kill him."

Schmidt laughed, "Yes, a brilliant plan. You're too popular to remove from your position. And if the Kaiser ordered your death? Well, there would be questions and problems. Morale in the military and the population would collapse if the High Command moved against you. But if you were assassinated by our enemies, a British secret service operation conducted by a French whore, well, our people would be so inflamed that victory on the battlefield would be all but assured."

Mata appeared to be staring at the man, but she silently studied everything in the room. She needed a

87

weapon. And then it struck her, she was a weapon. Her fists, feet, even her own sexuality; every part of her had been trained to kill.

"Major," she said and slowly, seductively, rolled off the bed. Standing, her nude form was the focus of every man in the train car as she stepped closer to Schmidt. "How did you know I wouldn't kill the General?"

Overconfident in his position, Schmidt began talking. "I didn't know. But as a precaution, I had the guards moved away from the train car, citing the General's need for privacy with his expensive whore. Then we stayed behind to observe. I'd had this car rigged with peep holes to keep an eye on you, as well as listen in on your conversations."

When she got a little too close, he raised the pistol.

She snickered and turned on her heels, showing herself off to both of the officers. "I'm obviously unarmed. Are you really afraid of me? Like you said," she swallowed and tried to say the word without flinching, "I'm a whore. I have no allegiance to any country or to any man. My body can belong to anyone if he pays the price."

The second officer grunted, "Maybe we should keep her for a while. I wouldn't mind…"

Schmidt turned with a disgusted look on his face. "Shut up, Mads."

The momentary distraction was what Mata counted on. Her right hand moved in a blur, grabbing Schmidt's right wrist and twisting. Stepping forward, she wrapped her right leg around his and using her weight, pulled him around and back. Before he knew what was happening, he had fallen back against her, facing his friend.

Mata's hand left his wrist and grabbed at his hand, forcing a finger into the trigger guard. Before Schmidt knew what was happening, two shots fired, striking Mads in the chest.

Mata could not hold him up for long, and the two of them fell back to the floor. The man's weight knocked the breath from her. His arms thrashed their way loose from her grip, and he gave a sharp elbow to her chest.

Pain blasted through her, and she did not react fast enough as the man rolled off her, coming up on his knees and pressing the pistol against her forehead.

"Any last words?" Schmidt asked.

"Yes. I am not a whore, but you? What you do for the Kaiser, that makes you a special kind of whore and a murderer."

Schmidt smiled and nodded. His fingers flexed. Mata was deafened by the gunshot. Fresh blood splattered onto her face and she shrieked. Then she opened her eyes.

The man released the weapon and fell to the side with a fresh bullet hole in his forehead.

"Are you alright, my dearest?" Kripker asked, wielding a pistol in one hand.

She looked up into his eyes. "You know that you're the only man I've ever loved."

He smiled and nodded. "Yes. I do know."

A moan came from the man Schmidt had called Mads. Kripker stepped to the man and took his pistol.

"He'll live. I'd like him alive. He needs to tell others this story. We can use it to force the Kaiser's hand and end this damned war," Kripker said as he stood. Grabbing his pants, he quickly put them on and added, "I'll call in the guards to clean up this mess. You, my dear, need to wipe that blood off of you and put something on."

Snatching her bag as he left, she tossed it on the bed and pulled out a long silk robe. Moments later, the train car filled with soldiers, carrying out the body of Schmidt and first treating Mads and then removing him.

The whole process seemed to take no time at all, finally leaving Kripker and Mata alone.

"Mata, the washroom is back there. You still have a little blood on your face and neck."

She put a hand to her face, "I thought I got it all. I'll be right back." Glancing down, she saw that drops of blood had seeped into the robe. "Damn."

As she stepped into the tiny room, she called out to him, "Otto, in my bag is a cigarette case. Would you light one up for me? I desperately need it after the last couple of days."

"Of course, love."

Grabbing a small towel, she washed herself. Looking in the mirror, she felt uneasy about something but was unsure why. Something about the silence in the other room bothered her, and she yelled out, "Did you find them?"

When she got no reply, she stepped out. Her heart sank at the scene before her. A lit cigarette awaited her in a crystal ashtray on the nightstand. Kripker lay on the bed, partially propped up by pillows. The man wore a peaceful expression, eyes closed and a smile on his face. His hands lay on his stomach, with a smoldering cigar nestled between his fingers. The metal tube that Gertrude had given her lay empty at his side.

The world felt like it dropped out from under her. Tears began to flow, followed by a primal scream of pain and rage.

"No. After all this. Why?"

She dropped to her knees, laid her head on the mattress, and wept. Her hand reached out to him one last time before the officers re-entered the car. She looked up at their shocked and saddened faces.

"Please give me one more moment with him." She moved the cigar and held his hand in hers. "Oh, Otto. The world should have been ours. Our personal playground. Au revoir, my general."

D. Alan Lewis

Part 4: Aftermath

"More coffee, Madame?" The waiter asked.

When she gave a nod, he topped off her cup. A sugar cube was tossed in, as well as a dash of cream. Life on the streets of Paris surrounding her favorite little café were just as she had left them two months earlier. Yet she could not find the happiness here that had always embraced her each morning.

A familiar voice called to her. "Good morning, Mata."

It came from behind her. Causally setting her cup down, she looked back over her shoulder.

"Mr. Black. I see you decided to come looking for me. Not that I've been hiding." She looked at the folded newspaper, laying on the table. Her picture along with a notice that the great Mata Hari had returned from her travels and would be performing again that night, were printed in bold ink.

Black walked around the table but to Mata's delight, Bonnie strolled beside him. Snatching a pair of unused chairs from other tables, he positioned them across from her and the visitors took their seats.

"You got the letter I sent?" Mata asked and watched Black nod. "Everything that happened was in there. Kripker's innocence, the Kaiser's plans, and all the deceit in between."

"Yes, yes. All the deceit," Black whispered.

She could tell that something bothered him. "Monsieur, the man is dead. It's what you wanted, oui?"

"We were all played, Mata. You said so yourself. Kripker was pushing for peace, not a continuation of this conflict. The war-mongers in Berlin got what they wanted; they silenced a popular voice calling for peace."

"No. Things didn't go as planned, did they?" Mata replied. "That Major who betrayed Otto died. And the doctors said Otto's heart gave out, so he didn't die at the hands of a British agent."

Black shook his head. "The Kaiser and his minions lost the edge they were counting on. They needed to create an uproar in Germany about the treachery of the British. It would have rallied their war-ravaged population into demanding a renewed war-effort instead of calling for peace. Instead, their nation mourns the loss of a hero from natural causes."

From his jacket pocket, he extracted a thick envelope and placed it on the table. With a gentle push, he moved it beside Mata's coffee cup.

"Consider this a recompense for your time, efforts, and the unfair actions we used to bully you into committing your deeds," he said and glanced to Bonnie. "And as promised, I gave our friend here the choice of staying in England or joining you here in Paris."

"There was no choice, was there, my pet?" Mata said, and smiled as Bonnie's face lit up.

"No, none at all, Madame."

Black stood. "Ladies, if you'll excuse me, the Crown has other work for me to do." He turned to leave but quickly added, "Mata, after this is all over, this war..." he paused and smiled. "I'd love to attend one of your performances." He paused and laughed. "With my wife in attendance, of course."

"Goodbye, Mr. Black. Something tells me our paths will cross again." Mata sipped at her coffee and looked at the young redhead. Bonnie's silky hair glowed in the sunlight. For the first time since she had left for the mission, Mata felt happy.

"I'll be performing tonight and there are a thousand things we must do to prepare."

"Sounds like a lot of work," Bonnie said.

"When it is something you love, it is never work, mon amour. Come, let's get started."

About the Author

In 1965, an object fell from space, somewhere near Kecksburg, PA. This was the same year that Alan was born. To date, no connection has been made between the two events but that hasn't stopped the conspiracy theorists and his children from speculating.

His latest project is the paranormal-noir *Voodoo Rumors* book series that debuted in February 2018. The series deals with all the unholy creatures of the night, including vampires, werewolves, demons, and ex-wives.

Alan's debut novel, a fantasy murder mystery, *The Blood in Snowflake Garden,* was a finalist for the 2010 Claymore Award and has been optioned for a TV series. He has several novels in print, along with over thirty shirt stories.

His novella, *Keely,* and steampunk short story, *The Celeste Affair,* were both winners in their categories in the 2015 Preditors & Editors Reader's Favorites Poll.

Find updates on his work at www.dalanlewis.com or www.voodoorumors.com

Made in the USA
Monee, IL
29 March 2022